BLOOD ON THE BIGHORNS

CARSON MCCLOUD

1

Brett Rawlins stretched out a scraped and bloodied hand toward the mottled gray boulder ahead. As they had for the past hour, his fingers fell short, and painfully he drove them into the damp ground, straining to drag himself forward. The fingers of both hands were mangled and twisted from his efforts. Black earth, coarse and gritty, clung to bleeding nails.

Every move hurt. Every breath burned hotter than a blacksmith's bellows.

Lowering his face into the dirt, Brett paused to rest. Clumps of damp soil clung against his cheek. Little light remained in the day now and, despite his own warmth, the pebble-dotted ground was cold beneath him.

His wounds still bled. Not counting what he'd done to his fingers, he'd been shot three times before he fell—once in the back, twice through his right arm with one bullet hitting near the shoulder and the other down at the elbow. These were beyond pain now. The numb flesh around them only tingled.

A blessing...all things considered. I wouldn't be able to move at all if I felt the whole of it.

Brett tilted his head to one side so he could look up at the steep walls of the crevasse. The cloudy autumn sky was fading from a featureless slate-grey to an impenetrable black.

Rain or snow tonight and I won't live to see morning. Even a heavy frost might do it.

Curled up at the edges like tiny boats, a handful of yellow aspen leaves slowly drifted down from above. They rode their thin currents to and fro, mocking him as they landed with gentle grace.

His own fall hadn't been so delicate. His clothing was still wet, he'd landed in a shallow pool, shattering the water's thin layer of icy skin and drenching himself from the waist down.

Likely the pool saved my life, if I'd struck a rock it would all be over now. But that won't be much comfort tonight when the cold comes.

For a moment Brett closed his eyes to rest. He tried to remember the last time he'd been warm. His mind felt foggy. His thoughts came thick and clumsy. For a brief moment he felt weightless as if his pains and struggles were many miles away, and then one thought—one name—screamed at him.

Allie.

His eyes shot open. Like a roaring bull, the pain crashed in. *Can't rest now. I need to get warm. I need to save Allie.*

He reached out again, and this time his fingertips brushed over the rough boulder. Brett almost smiled. He couldn't remember how long he'd been dragging himself along. If he could use the boulder to push himself upright, he might be able to walk or crawl and at the very least he could get sitting upright where he might be able to stop the bleeding.

Maybe even get a fire going.

Slowly, Brett pulled his way closer and then, after a few minutes effort, he twisted around until he had his back propped up against the boulder.

He caught up a handful of the mocking aspen leaves as they floated near. There was a small pile of twigs and grassy debris packed in tight along the boulder's base and he scooped out what he could. Then he piled up the thinnest slivers of wood and grass along with the leaves into a little nest. He laid a few of the larger twigs on top.

Digging through his pocket he found flint and steel. At first his fingers fumbled over each; it hurt just to bend them. He couldn't afford to fail now. To live through the night he needed a fire. He willed them steady, ignored the pain, focused his thoughts, then stuck the pair until his knuckles bled and a lucky spark landed in the bristling nest.

Gently, he lifted the nest up and breathed life into it.

Smoke and then flame bloomed from the nest's heart. Brett set it atop a pile of larger sticks and held his hands over the growing fire—front and then back—melting the hair from his hands. He didn't care. He had to get warm. His whole body rattled with cold.

A branch, thick as his arm and long as an axehandle, lay nearby. He leaned out to grab it, ignoring the burst of pain in his back.

Feeling was returning to his fingers and he ran them over the worn wood. Otherwise smooth, it was pitted and scarred in a few places, likely from beating itself against the rocks. During a mountain storm rainwater would fill this crevasse with thousands upon thousands of gallons, all crashing down from the Bighorns like Moses dropping the Red Sea.

His mother, Betsy, had always loved that story, though she'd been partial to the New Testament with its forgiveness and turning of the other cheek. Jim, his father, had been Old Testament fire and brimstone through and through. There had always been a twinkle in the old man's eye when the waters swallowed up the Pharaoh's chariots. Folks spoke of Jim Rawlins as a hard man—and he was once—in the time before mother died.

Now he was buried beside Brett's mother on the little hill that overlooked their home. Once a promised land of milk and honey on par with Canaan itself, Wyoming hadn't been kind to the Rawlins family. Twelve years his parents scratched out a living at the base of the Bighorns. Twelve long years of roaring mountain floods, blizzards, stillborn calves, hard-luck heifers, lightning, drought, thieves or rustlers, wolves preying on the newborn calves, backbreaking work, and finally disease.

Brett's mother had passed first. Died of the yellow fever three winters ago. Over two dozen others down south in Pryor had gotten it, Pastor Covey and his family, the Dugans who ran a big sprawling ranch south of town, the Chantrys, and more. Half of those who caught it died. Betsy Rawlins had been in that half. Brett and his father buried her in the springtime right after the ground thawed.

Brett and his father had soldiered on with ranch business, but without the love of his life, Jim Rawlins was a changed man. He'd grown ever more morose and moody. He'd done less and less around the place as Brett took up as much of his father's burdens as he could. Finally, two months back Jim Rawlins hanged himself, one final Wyoming tragedy.

Well the final one until today, Brett sighed.

He had been the one to find his father's body, swinging beneath the big cottonwood halfway to town. He hadn't seen it coming, if anything father seemed better in his last few months, like the veil was lifting just a bit. Brett told no one the truth of his father's passing. Instead he made up a story about getting caught unprepared in a late blizzard on the mountain. Sheriff Payson had asked a few questions when he reported it, but he'd gone along with Brett's lie easy enough. Such things happened often enough, and if Payson suspected the truth he hadn't confronted Brett over it.

On his own, Brett buried his father right next to his mother. And since then he'd been on the ranch alone.

Looks like I'll be joining them soon enough. Only who'll come along and bury me?

Brett eyed the high rocky ledges all around him. No one would ever find his body. Even the wolves and buzzards wouldn't climb down the crevasse to gnaw on him. The thought almost made him smile. He imagined the drooling beasts smelling him but having no way to reach him.

He ran his hands over the axehandle branch again, debating what to do with it. On one hand it would make a decent crutch. From here it looked like the crevasse wound its way down the mountain and sooner or later there had to be a place where he might crawl out. By leaning on the branch he would have a better chance at staying on his feet. On the other hand he could get a lot of warmth by burning it and he couldn't see much else lying about. Not close anyway. Maybe he could use it to reach another piece of wood. He craned his neck around, searching.

Without seeing anything useful, he leaned back against the boulder. His hands and the left side of his body were warmer now, and he realized just how exhausted he really was.

So very tired.

His heavy eyes slipped shut. In the cold dark Brett's mind drifted. He hadn't planned on any of this. Today wasn't supposed to go anything like this. He'd just gone out riding with Allie.

The day had been clear and bright with only a few low clouds scattered on the far western horizon. Around the ranch the land was still green, but summer's blaze peaked months ago and the mountain air whispered the barest promise of another bitter Wyoming winter. The Bighorn peaks thrust up to the east and made a backdrop of gray arrowheads jutting across the pale blue sky. In a few shadowed pockets a froth of white snow could still be seen, faded remnants of the prior winter. Soon enough though the drifts would start piling up again as the peaks put on their snowy mantles.

The ranch lay nestled down in the foothills, running from the grassy flatlands all the way up into the high timber and then the Bighorns themselves. Most of the cattle were still up near the peaks, fattening up in the high lush meadows, but soon he'd have to push them down. In Wyoming, winter was always near.

"Catch me if you can," Allie had said. She wore her hair loose—flowing back in an inviting river of dark brown waves—and raced out ahead of him. She leaned down close against her chestnut's neck and spurred the gelding on faster.

"I'll have you in a jiffy," Brett laughed as he kicked his mare after her.

Allie turned back and flashed him a brilliant smile. One that made his heart skip a beat.

God she is pretty.

Allie led Brett east climbing ever higher toward the craggy old peaks. Grazing in the lower pasture, the ranch's prized red stallion, Cimarron, watched them, gave a disdainful snort, and then went back to his mares.

Of the two he was by far the better rider—he practically lived in the saddle—but she was a good bit lighter and her chestnut could run for days. They'd ridden past Lookout Point and Bald Knob, and then curled around toward Ironwood Springs, where he'd finally caught her. He scooped her off her saddle, tucking her against his chest and holding her close.

"Brett Rawlins you are a scoundrel," she teased in his arms.

"If I'm a scoundrel, we're a pair. You're wild as any mustang."

She play-slapped him with her riding gloves, then kissed him.

Brett felt his mother's ring in the front pocket of his jeans. Ever since they'd met all those years ago at the little one-room school-house over on Shell Creek Allie Smith had been his girl. From the time they were ten years old their parents always expected them to marry, and they were used to being teased about it.

Then for a time they slowly drifted apart.

After his mother died, Brett had been needed at the ranch and he hadn't seen Allie more than once or twice whenever he and his father had gone to her parent's store in Pryor for supplies. Then a week after his father's death she'd ridden out one day to tell him how sorry she was to hear about his loss.

From then on Allie made a point to visit him at least once a week. They'd go riding or just sit around the house talking about people they both knew or trips they'd like to take someday. She would bring lunch or cook for him, and she was a good cook. She'd talk about how much she wanted to go to San Francisco or New York and stay in fancy hotels. Brett's own dreams were smaller; in truth he wasn't sure what he wanted. He'd heard the Crow Indians had a big Medicine Wheel up in the mountains. He'd like to ride up and see it one day. Allie teased him about his simple dreams. She always asked him what he would do with his father's ranch. He never had a good answer.

His father and mother had expected him to stick it out and reap the rewards of their hard work. Many times they'd told him the ranch would one day prosper. That day never felt any closer though, and Brett never felt like he had a choice in the matter.

He had been riding around with the ring for two weeks now, trying to find the right moment to ask Allie to marry him. Wrapped up in his arms, she stared up at him with her large brown eyes. Her lips parted. His mouth went dry.

"Allie, I want to ask you something. Allie I—"

"Well if this ain't sweet. Two young lovers out for a little ride. Why I bet they even got a picnic lunch in those saddlebags."

Brett turned his horse toward the voice. Immediately, he recognized the man who'd spoken.

Kip Lane was young, less than twenty, like Brett himself. He was dressed in his usual dark tailored jacket and his black curly hair hung down to his collar. His beard and mustache were neatly trimmed. Beneath his black hat his midnight eyes shown hard and cruel.

Lane had showed up in Pryor last winter, riding for Davis Judd. Judd had bought up the old Dugan place, moved in, and instantly become one of the biggest ranchers in Wyoming. Just a week later Lane killed a pair of men over a card game. He had a reputation as a man quick with a gun, and he took every excuse to use it.

Kip wasn't alone either. There were three other Judd riders with him.

"I believe you're right Kip," one of them said. The man spat a load of tobacco and leaned heavy on his pommel. He grinned at Allie. "I shore would like to have me a picnic with that little filly."

"We aren't looking for trouble," Brett said. "Just out for a ride."

"Why so are we," Kip said with a wide smile. He spread his arms. "We're out for a little ride of our own. Saw you racing up the mountain and thought we'd swing over and say howdy. You know, I've seen that girl of yours all over town. She sure is a pert one."

He leered at Allie and winked.

Brett wasn't a gunfighter and he knew it. His mother hated guns and until his father died, he'd never carried anything more than a long rifle for hunting. He'd certainly never drawn his gun on another man, nor needed to, but he was wearing his father's big Colt. A thought came to him then.

This meeting is no accident.

No one ever rode up this way. Lane and his men had been waiting for them and they aimed to get Allie. She knew it too. He felt her arms tighten around him. His father's Colt was on his right side, pinned beneath her legs and he'd have to pitch her off to reach it. He didn't want to put her afoot, but they couldn't escape and the only chance to save her was with the pistol.

"I think that little firebrand is more woman than a home-spun boy like you can handle. Maybe you ought to leave her here with us," Kip said. "We'll take good care of her."

Brett's father had long ago taught him to act when needed. The words echoed out to him. *There's a time for talking and a time for doing, and when it's time for doing act before the other man does. Don't ever give him a chance to move first.*

With his left hand Brett pushed Allie off his horse or rather he tried to. As soon as he tensed he felt her arms squeeze hard around him, holding him fast. A bullet struck him in the shoulder and another burned along his right arm at the elbow. Allie's arms flung wide and she came free then, tumbling away.

She's been hit, Brett's mind screamed. He couldn't see any blood on her though. He looked back at Lane. *If I don't fight now we'll both die.*

Brett tried to draw the Colt, but his wounded arm refused to move. He had to stop these men. Somehow he had to save Allie. More shots rang out. Frightened by the shooting, his mare wheeled and ran. They raced straight for a deep crevasse and would have fallen in, if Brett hadn't whipped the reins around just before the crazed beast plunged over. He had to get back to Allie and help her escape. She couldn't outrun so many.

The mare crow-hopped as another shot rang out, Brett felt the bullet slam into his back and then he fell...for a long time he fell... and he remembered only darkness and pain before waking up in the icy pool.

Brett jerked awake with a start. He couldn't remember falling asleep, he'd only closed his eyes for a moment, but the crevasse was dark now, no light remaining in the cloudy sky, not even a single star.

His fire was burned down to ash. A few of the leaves and a handful of grass had scattered and he piled them up for fuel. Leaning over as best he could, he blew on the coals until coaxing out a tiny flame. He fed a few more of his precious twigs to the fire and it blazed a little brighter.

His father's Colt still hung against his hip; the leather thong had held it in place. He thought the powder was still dry. He didn't believe it had fallen in the water. His knife too remained on his belt, and he used it to shave a few slivers off his walking branch and then fed them to the growing fire.

With the new light he saw another branch laying off to his left and, with the axehandle, he dragged it closer. This branch was bigger, gnarled and ancient and thick. He centered it over the fire and added a few more shavings to help it catch.

He ran his hands over the boulder and felt spongy wet moss on one side. He tore some free and brought it around to his mouth to lick at the moisture. His canteen was still on the mare, likely miles away by now. He looked up at the steep walls of his prison again.

And even if she isn't, even if she's at the top of this hole that water might as well be a thousand miles off. I'll never climb out of here.

The wound in his back was bleeding again; he could feel a new prickle of dampness spreading under his shirt. He reached back and packed a handful of the moss around the wound as best he could manage. It wasn't the cleanest thing, but it might keep him from bleeding to death.

He warmed himself by the growing fire. He needed to find Allie. He'd failed to keep her safe from Lane, but he could still rescue her. Tomorrow he'd have to follow the course of the water and see if he could find a way out.

Tomorrow, if I make it through the night.

———

"Mr. Judd, I've no interest in selling," Brett said.

"Are you sure?" Davis Judd said. His eyes, green almost to the point of being yellow and a little small despite his narrow face, darted around from the snug little cabin to the corral, and then the barn, taking it all in. "Place like this will take a lot of work, before it comes to something."

He studied Brett again, flashing a wry smile. "If I were a young man like yourself I would want to see the world before settling down. There's a lot out there in the world, and with what I'm offering you could go anywhere."

Brett studied the shorter man.

Davis Judd wasn't from the west. He was from Illinois and last year he'd moved in after buying out the Dugan place, not long before Brett's father had died. His gaze skipped from the house to the barn again. Idly, he scratched the thin, brown beard along his chin and neck.

"I might could offer you a bit more. Say another two thousand?" Davis smiled again, a hair warmer this time. The skin crinkled into a web of fine lines around those small eyes. He gestured with his gloves. "Your stock is good and fat. I could sell them at a small profit. Two thousand more would set a young man like yourself up very well. You could even buy a better property. One far nicer than this."

"Look Mr. Judd," Brett said. "This was my father's dream. He worked his whole life for it, him and ma both. I can't let it go. This is where I grew up."

"Now I know what you're thinking," Davis jumped in. "You're thinking if there's better land available why don't I buy it myself." He smacked the riding gloves into his empty palm. "Well this piece fits in real nice with what I already own. It's a good match for me you see?"

"I appreciate your offer but I just can't sell. This was my father's place and he wanted me to have it," Brett said.

"Ahh, I understand. When my own father died he left me a freight business back east," Davis looked out toward the mountains. He leaned in a little closer to Brett, "I hated it. So I sold out first chance I got and came west. A man can be big out here, but only if he's strong enough. If he's strong he can be as big as his desires. He can tame this wild land and become a king."

For a time neither spoke. Davis only studied him with a pinched expression. Finally, he put the gloves back on. He looked toward the little graveyard just above the ranch.

"Well, I understand. It is difficult to sell something your father and mother worked so hard for. Something they dreamed of handing down to you. I'll tell you what though. If you change your mind. If you decide that your father's dreams aren't for you and you have plans of your own. Come find me. My offer will stay open," Judd said. His face had slipped a notch, the smile not so bright, nor the green eyes so friendly.

He looked like a wolf studying a young elk. Without another word, he mounted his buckboard and then rolled back toward Pryor.

Leaning on the fence near the corral, Brett watched him go. Then he turned to his parent's graves and beyond, staring for a long time at the far horizon and the rising mountains. Why was he holding on so tight to his father's dream?

He thought about the offer. It was a lot of money. More than he'd see in many years ranching for himself.

Allie would want me to take it. She spoke often of seeing the world. San Francisco, New York, Paris even. To Brett these were just words, places full of too many people all crowded together. His parents took him to Denver once—years ago—to look at a pair of shorthorn breeding bulls. Brett had thought the city far too large. He couldn't see how people could breathe and grow if they were all pressed in shoulder-to-shoulder like that.

Still the decision wasn't Allie's; it was his. The ranch was the only thing he had left of his parents. Everything his father had ever worked for was tied up in land and cattle. All his father ever wanted was to pass it on to him. He couldn't sell it.

But is this what I really want? To be a simple rancher the rest of my life? Do I have to honor father's wishes?

He didn't have any answers.

2

Brett woke to a biting cold. Again his fire had burned down to orange coals and he added more of his precious fuel, hoping to drag it back to life. Above him the wind howled over the rocky edge of the crevasse. The sky was clear now; he looked at the narrow slice of distant white stars.

At least I'm down out of the wind.

The tiny fire gave him little true warmth, he had almost nothing left to burn, but he felt better just for watching the crackling yellow flames. After two hours the sun rose and the stars faded away into the blue.

With the axe-handle branch and more than a little pain, Brett managed to climb to his feet. He was dizzy. His head swam and he held the boulder to steady himself. It took several long minutes before his vision finally cleared.

"Got to get out of here," he mumbled. Using the branch as a cane, he forced one leg in front of the other and set off down the twisting watercourse.

Travel was painfully slow. He stopped often, careful always to stay propped against the wall or one of the bigger rocks scattered along his path.

In most places the crevasse was wider at the bottom than the top and the ground was covered with fine grainy sand mixed with small worn-down pebbles. Here and there he found piles of rough granite rocks and he struggled climbing over these. He fell once, cutting his palm over a jagged stone. For a few moments he laid where he'd fallen, staring at the wound dumbly and enjoying the warmth of the high sun on his face.

Lord, it feels good to let go for a time.

He thought about Allie then. About what Kip Lane and his men were doing to her. He had to get out of this damned hole. He had to save her somehow. He couldn't let her down. *Move or die*, he told himself.

Finally he gathered his feet, propped himself up with the branch, and then started off again.

The sun rose to its peak and Brett thought he'd covered at least two miles. Given the winding route and lack of landmarks, it was impossible to tell for sure. An hour further along the crevasse joined with another—there were many such in the broken country near the mountains—and then widened considerably. Then his course snaked off toward the south and west.

"This should come out along Bitter Creek," Brett muttered. His voice, cracked and coarse like an old man's, startled him.

He shuffled on through the afternoon, and soon the shadows drew in tight around him. He paused to take in the warmth whenever the path turned or was just wide enough to allow a window of sunshine down.

Toward evening he came to a clear shallow pool almost as wide as the crevasse. He bent down eagerly and drank from it. The water tasted a hint brackish but he was too thirsty to care, and afterward he rested against a rocky shelf. He was about to move on when he noticed several deer tracks in the thick mud around the pool.

If the deer can get down here there must be a way out.

He began searching for where the deer had come or gone. But the shadows were growing deep now and he couldn't find it.

Much as he didn't want to spend a second night down here, there was no help for it. The water had bought him some time at least. All he needed now was a fire.

He found a brace of wood where the surging stormwater had trapped it between two boulders, and that night he kept warm. He felt a little stronger—his wounds finally stopped bleeding—but his empty stomach rumbled. He was warm and he'd found water, but he needed to eat.

In the morning's light, Brett followed the tracks down until they vanished in a patch of pea gravel. The gravel went on for a ways but at the far end there were no tracks.

The deer aren't coming down this far. The way out must be close.

He returned to the middle of the gravel and studied the rocky walls all around him. He saw nothing at first, then a tuft of fur hanging from a rock. He moved closer. There was a place where the deer must have scrambled up along a worn trail between two rocks and finally out over a little notch at the top. Using the axe-handle for support, he started up.

The path was tricky, very narrow and sharp rocks dug at his legs and torso with every step.

He paused in a wide spot just below the notch to catch his breath and study the final obstacle. There was a slight bend in the trail ahead and then it narrowed even more at the end. Looking at it he wasn't completely sure he could manage it. The deer must have had his own problems as more tufts of coarse brown hair were snagged on the rocky wall.

"No help for it," Brett said and started forward.

The rock bit at his hands and arms and back as he began squeezing down into the notch. His chest caught and he breathed out as he could to gain another inch. He held his breath until his lungs burned then inhaled and was sure he'd gotten himself completely stuck. He reached out with an arm to pull himself along, but found only empty space. Panic rose in him and as he took a breath his chest pressed tighter against the rock.

I'm going to die here. I should have kept following the water down, sooner or later there had to be a better place to escape.

He reached out ahead again. There had to be something to grab on to. He felt his axe handle branch where he'd dropped it. He picked it up and spun it sideways to wedge between the rocks, then he strained and pushed until it bowed. Then without warning he popped clear and fell.

Brett had never been happier to fall flat on his face. He was free. For the first time in two days, he was out of those dark hellish depths. He was up on the grasslands with the wind over his face. He breathed deep, enjoying the sweet open air and taking in the wide expanse of perfect sky. Finally, he climbed to his feet and took his bearings.

Still in the Bighorn foothills, Ironwood springs lay a few miles to the north, Bitter creek five or six miles south. The ranch house was close, due west and less than half as far.

Using the branch for support, Brett headed for home. He was almost there when he saw the first faint tendrils of smoke curl up from his father's chimney.

Who could be at the house?

Allie, she escaped. She must have gotten to her horse while they were chasing after me. Maybe she had the Sheriff and a posse with her and they were out looking for him. Some of them might be at the cabin. Brett almost let out a cheer. Soon Kip Lane would be run out of the country. Westerners would not tolerate a man who abused women.

Despite the stiffness of his wounds, Brett picked up his pace. There was a thick grove of white spruce between himself and the house. He crashed through the underbrush, startling a small cottontail from its morning feeding.

His mouth watered at the thought of a fat roasted rabbit, but there was plenty of food at the house. Smoked ham, beef, potatoes, canned vegetables from his mother's garden. Food he wouldn't have to chase, kill, and clean.

He paused at the grove's edge, catching his breath and watching the house. For a moment he just took it in. He'd never missed the place so much.

Allie will be so happy to see me.

He felt his mother's ring still tucked in his pants pocket. There was a full-time preacher down in Pryor. He'd walk in, ask her to marry him, and tomorrow they would be husband and wife. His mother's dress was stored in the big leather-bound trunk at the foot of his parent's bed. This would all be like some bad dream or a wild story they told their children one day.

Then he noticed there were extra horses in the corral, along with his own, and Allie's. The unknown horses all wore the 9O brand of Davis Judd.

Why would the posse all be riding Judd's horses?

The outhouse door opened with a bang. Adjusting his pants and suspenders, a greasy man wearing a dirty, yellow shirt and a mop of long curly red hair stepped out. Brett recognized him almost instantly. One of Kip Lane's friends. One of the men who'd shot him.

The red-haired man dropped his cigarette on the porch, wiped his mouth on his sleeve, and disappeared into the house.

Brett's heart pounded; his breathing quickened. *Kip Lane and his friends are at my father's house. They are using my mother's stove and my mother's pots and my mother's stove.* Brett's hand fell to his father's Colt. He drew the gun and found his wounded arm could barely lift it. Worse, his fingers were mangled and stiff and he had to concentrate just to move them. He couldn't fight like this. He passed the pistol over to his left hand. This hand too had been hurt when he'd dragged himself along, but the fingers weren't so bad off.

What to do next though?

If he struck with surprise he might get several of them. He was a good shot, though not very experienced with the pistol. He knew the layout of the house. He knew where the blind spots were. He could kill these men. First though, he needed to get to the back of the barn. From there he could slip around closer to the house. Maybe break out a window and fire inside.

I have to find Allie too and get her out of harm's way. Hopefully she's already escaped. The fact that Kip Lane and his men were at his father's ranch wasn't promising though. Likely Allie was trapped in there with them.

He slipped his way through the spruce to the back of the barn.

The boards were painted red and pressed together tight. His father had been particularly proud of that. Three months he'd worked at fitting them just right to block the cold Wyoming wind out.

The front door of the house opened; it struck roughly against the wall. Brett cringed.

How dare they break my mother's house.

Brett squeezed the Colt tight. With his other hand he cocked the hammer back and leaned one eye around the barn's corner. When he saw who it was he froze.

Allie.

They had caught her. His worst fears were confirmed. There wouldn't be a posse or any other help, Lane still held her here. She crossed to the corral. Her face held no expression and her long brown locks swirled around her face, catching the wind. Her cheeks were flush and the top of her blouse had been opened at the neck.

I've got to get her away from here. Away from that bastard Kip Lane. But how? If she came to him now they could grab a horse and ride for Pryor. The law would help them.

"Al—" Brett started.

"Hey sweet thing," Kip Lane's voice came from inside the house. He stepped out onto the porch and rested his arms on the railing, "I'm not done with you yet."

Allie turned back toward the house and away from Brett. "I'm not done with you yet either." She ran to Lane then and leapt up into his arms; she wrapped him tight around the neck and began kissing him.

Kip laughed between kisses. He ran his hands through Allie's flowing hair.

"What am I going to do with you?" Lane said.

"Whatever you want," Allie laughed.

Brett felt his knees weaken. Retreating from the edge, he put his back to the barn and sagged down against the boards. Two days he'd fought his way through hell and back to save Allie. Two miserable days. And now he'd found her kissing the very man who'd shot him.

"Let's go back inside," Lane said. "Maybe you can cook me up something to eat."

"I thought I heard a noise out here," Allie said.

"Nothing out here but the damn wind," Lane laughed. "Maybe a wolf or two waiting to eat a sweet little girl like you."

"I'll show you sweet little girl," she said.

The door banged shut and again Brett leaned out to look. They were back inside now. He could hear them in his parent's house, laughing. He wanted to kill them all. He could cross to the house, break out a window, and fire inside. The idea was crazy. With Lane inside, along with the others who'd jumped him, he'd never stand a chance.

He wasn't like these men. He wasn't a gunfighter. Until now his life had prepared him for ranching, not gunplay. With luck he might get one or two, but luck would only carry him so far. He couldn't run. Not wounded as he was. With his fingers stiff and broken he doubted he could even reload the pistol, and for all he knew the bullets had been soaked and wouldn't fire anyway.

They'll kill me for sure.

His horse, still saddled, stood idle in the corral. Brett eased back behind the barn and around the opposite side to the corral's corner. Last summer his father had asked him to replace the post there only he'd never quite gotten around to it. It was loose and half-rotted just below ground. Brett pushed against the post until it cracked a little, and then pulled back with all his strength. The wood groaned and protested. Brett strained harder. He brought his feet close to the post's base and leaned his bodyweight against it. The post cracked again and popped. Then it slipped almost a foot at the top and the highest rail of the corral fell away loose, followed by the second.

For a moment Brett froze—Colt in hand—praying the noise wouldn't bring anyone out of the house.

Brett's mare was close. Lane's men hadn't even bothered to unsaddle her. He'd fed that mare by hand often enough and when he held out his open hand she crossed over to him. She sniffed at the sleeves of his shirt. Her eyes rolled. She started back, not liking the smell of his blood, but Brett let go of the post and snatched up her bridle. He led her out over the bottom rail and around behind the barn, out of view from the house.

Brett started out for the shelter of the trees on foot, always keeping the barn between himself and the cabin.

Once he was deep in the spruce, he mounted up. His back and right arm sent lances of hot pain surging through him. He struggled not to cry out. Mercifully, the pain subsided.

Now where to go?

Pryor was the obvious choice—he could explain everything to the Sheriff—but it was also the first place they'd look when they realized he'd gotten his horse back. They might even catch him on the way to town. Despite a head start, he couldn't outrun them. A hard ride in the saddle wasn't an option. He needed a place to hole up, somewhere to get food and rest and recover. Someplace known to no one and up in the wild country near the peaks.

The old mine shack.

Brett's father had bought the ranch off a miner after the man decided to go back to Montana. Though he seldom went to that corner of the ranch he knew exactly where the mine was. They'd lived in the little shack for a few months while building the ranch house proper down in the lower foothills. It lay well off the trails in the remote country near the mountains. A tough place to find.

And one not known to Allie.

The mine shack was solid too with a steady source of water flowing from a spring, and situated as it was, you could see out for a good distance. His father had once stored some hardtack and dried meat there along with a few canned goods in case they were ever trapped up that way during a lightning storm or blizzard.

He could hide out there for a few days, recover, and then decide what to do.

———

IN THE LATE afternoon the wind shifted direction, coming out of the north now and turning colder as the sun brushed over the western horizon. One final golden wave swept over the foothills and bathed the towering Bighorns in a hundred shades of orange and red and violet.

Brett rubbed his arms and breathed into his hands. The movement did little to warm him, but there was nothing else to be done.

He found the old mine just as the last wink of sunlight faded.

Like a calf leaning on its mother for warmth, the lonely structure pressed right up tight against the mountain. It was perfect for his purposes. From the front windows a man could see out all over the country, but the way it was built into the mountain and with the building's faded gray exterior it almost impossible to spot. Originally, the miner had built his small home against an outcropping of granite and—as he had later enclosed the shaft as well—it served as both house and mine entrance. Brett tied his horse up to a pine sapling near the corral.

"Sorry girl, but I can't afford for you to go running off tonight," he apologized. It wasn't his way to leave a horse haltered overnight; she'd already spent two nights that way. There was an old fenced pen nearby, but in the dark he couldn't see what kind of shape it was in. The last thing he needed was to be stranded without a horse. "Tomorrow, I'll find a way to let you loose."

He unbuckled his saddle letting it fall and then dragging both it and his saddlebags to the shack.

His father had nailed a wide board across the door and Brett pried it loose. He opened the door, lifting when it sagged against the rotted leather the miner had used for hinges.

Inside and out of the wind the air felt warmer. Save for a table, two chairs, and a neat stack of wood, the place was both clean and empty. In one corner there was a small cast iron stove. Brett put some old bits of tinder inside and soon had a fire going. He added a few of the larger logs from the pile in the corner. His stomach rumbled in protest. He couldn't remember the last time he'd eaten.

Opening his saddlebags he found the picnic food, a few apples, some cheese, bread, and a bit of smoked ham he'd bought in Youngston, all still good enough to eat.

Must not have bothered to search the bags. Well why would they with all the food in father's house.

He sat down near the stove and ate. Everything tasted a little strange but right now it was all he had. His canteen still hung on his saddle so he had plenty to drink. Only after it was all gone did he realize just how hungry he'd been.

The place wasn't nearly so solid as he'd remembered. Wind whistled through a number of cracks in the walls. Loose boards rattled on the roof.

The stove's warmth felt good on his back and though tired his mind refused to let him sleep. Dark thoughts plagued him.

Why did she do it? Did she know they planned on killing me?

"She must have," Brett said aloud. Allie hadn't held his arms out of fear, but to trap him where he couldn't fight back or ride away.

"How could she do this? And why? We've known each other since we were children."

The night held no answers.

Brett took his mother's ring from his pocket. The tiny diamond glistened in the firelight. Allie. How could she?

For a long time he only stared at it, then at last his chin drooped down against his chest and sleep claimed him.

Brett slept fitfully, his dreams dark and angry. Bits and pieces of the last few days came to him in jumbles. A smiling Kip Lane chasing after him, guns out and blazing, bullets whizzing by. Pain. Allie kissing him and then smiling and then laughing. And Falling. Falling into the deep bone-cutting cold.

The sun was nearly at its peak before he woke. He couldn't remember the last time he'd slept in past a sunrise much less to almost noon. His body was a solid bundle of knotted soreness. He stretched as best he could, and then set about to see what his father had left here.

Searching the shack, he found the few canned goods stored away, peaches and beans, a spare jacket, one of his father's by the size, too big across the chest and shoulders for himself, and a box of candles. The smoked meats were gone. Stolen by a rat or mouse no doubt. He ate a can of peaches, drank from his canteen, then took a small bucket and went down to the spring for water.

Except for where an aspen had fallen across it, the fence around the pen was in good shape. He piled some rough brush up around the fallen tree so his horse wouldn't try to escape and then turned the mare loose inside.

In the cabin again, he stripped off his bloody shirt. The material had stuck to the wounds in his arm and shoulder. They bled freely again once he took it off. He couldn't see the hole in his back, but it too felt like it was bleeding.

His arm felt feverish. If the wounds were infected, any of them, he might die.

I need help, real help. A doctor. But where?

Pryor was out of the question. He'd have to pass near the ranch house to get there and by now Lane would know the horse was gone; the gunman would surely have his friends out searching for him. Sheridan was less than a day's ride over the mountains. He knew a few places where he could cross, but they were all treacherous, especially this time of year. Getting caught in an early blizzard or just falling off his horse that high up would kill him as easy as a bullet. No Sheridan was out; he was in no shape for it. Not with the weather turning.

Youngston. It has to be Youngston.

The Mormon community was north and a little west of the ranch. He could ride there without being seen.

New as he was to the area and with the Mormons keeping to themselves, Lane wouldn't have any friends there. The Mormons were clannish in their dealings. They tended to avoid other settlers except in the direst of needs. They weren't a trusting lot, especially of outsiders.

Brett knew them through his parents who'd sold them several head of cattle when they first arrived and started their settlement. His father had taken a liking to their leader, Mr. Sweeney. Several times since then they'd driven down a beef or two whenever the Mormons needed it.

The Mormons knew medicine; they could take care of his wounds, certainly better than he could by himself. He thought they even had a doctor among their number. The Sweeney's would be able to help him.

Besides anything is better than waiting up here for fever to set in. All I have to do is reach them.

3

The day had only grown colder and night rushed in as he rode. Dark came early, the sky churning with low rolling clouds. A few fine white flakes stung against his cheek. Old man winter was trying to shoulder his way past Lady fall.

Brett pointed his horse north and west, toward Youngston, and hunched down in the saddle. Oversized as it was, his father's heavy jacket held back the worst of the cold, but the wind burned his exposed face and hands.

The weary mare struggled on, and Brett could not blame her. For the last few days she'd eaten nothing but browned late-season grass. She was used to hardship though—mountain born and raised—and the deep strength of her bloodline showed.

He'd eaten a can of warmed beans before leaving the cabin and was glad for the hot meal in his stomach.

The plodding of the mare's hooves clopped even and steady; Brett shook his head trying to fight off sleep. He was so tired. His head felt like a lead weight, only the bitter cold seemed to goad him onward.

Brett's mind drifted back to a time long ago when both his parents were alive.

He was back in their cabin. His mother stood at the stove in a blue plaid dress, stirring a beef stew to go along with the warm bread she'd baked earlier. He loved his mother's bread. The crust was always thick and usually she'd give him a taste of molasses or salted butter to go along with it.

Father sat at the table in the other room, cleaning his Colt with a rag and oil.

Done oiling the pistol, his father slid the shells back in their chambers with six heavy clicks. On each click mother's shoulders jerked. His mother hated the gun, hated all guns. Even as a child Brett had known that.

"I wish you wouldn't do that," she said when father was done. "I wish you'd put that back in the trunk or just get rid of it entirely."

"There's wolves in the mountains Betsy. With all the snow this year they've come down from the high places," father said. "If we don't stop them we'll lose half the calves."

"You have the rifle for that," mother said.

"When we ride Brett carries the rifle. I need this for myself. We can't afford to let the wolves take our herd. The future of the ranch, Brett's future, depends on it."

"You don't need that vile thing for anything."

"It's only for wolves, love. Only for the wolves."

Brett jerked awake and almost fell out of the saddle. He blinked. He grabbed the pommel with both hands fighting to keep himself upright. He squeezed it tight enough to make his hands hurt.

Was I dreaming? Can't do that again. Out here a fall from the saddle would surely kill me.

The dark was so thick now he couldn't see more than a few feet. Waves of snow flew in fine crystals. Tiny flakes scratched over his cheeks. So intense was the cold that they blew by without melting. He had no idea where he was or how far he'd come. He felt his mother's ring still in his pocket. He felt the weight of his father's Colt on his hip.

He kept riding. The only thing he knew for certain was that they were still heading downhill. There was a worn wagon trail between Youngston and Pryor. If he found it, he should be able to tell which way was north by its slope, and then he could just follow the trail up to the Sweeney's.

On through the night he rode until his tired mare slowed. He spurred her on. He studied the ground until his eyes hurt. What if he'd already crossed it? What if he was west of Youngston? There were few people in that direction just a smattering of cabins or dugouts, scattered far and wide, most long abandoned.

Brett's thoughts were foggy; the reins slipped through his fingers and fell. The mare stopped. Looking after the reins he thought he saw the worn ruts of the trail but couldn't be sure. It was so dark and cold. Clinging to the saddle, he slumped forward. He pulled on the horse's mane and swung her so she faced what he guessed was north. Then he popped his heels against her flanks, and felt the exhausted mare start walking again.

He fought to keep his head up and eyes open. He had to reach Youngston.

The ranch...I have to save the ranch for father. Just hold on. Hold on for a little bit longer.

————

"How do you feel?"

Brett tried lifting himself up on his elbow. Pain shot through his right arm and he slipped back immediately. He gazed around but everything was white and blurry. "Mmmm, sore," he croaked, "sore and tired."

"Good," the voice from earlier called. "That means you're alive."

"I made it then. How long—?" Brett asked. The words snagged like briars in his throat.

"Easy now. You are not well."

Brett's vision started to clear. A tall man loomed over him, blonde and thin, but not overly so.

"Mr. Sweeney?" he said. Somehow he'd made it to Youngston then.

"Please, call me Gideon. You showed up three nights ago, half froze, and..." Sweeney's voice trailed off. His questioning eyes fell on Brett's bandaged right arm.

"Shot."

"Yes," the older man nodded. "Any idea who did it?"

He held out a cup and Brett drank from it. The contents had a cinnamon and honey flavor and it was warm and soothing. His throat felt better the instant he swallowed.

"Kip Lane. Some friends of his too."

"He is a troubled young man."

"You know of him?"

"We do." Gideon hesitated. His eyes roamed over the rest of the room, and then he shifted his weight uncomfortably.

"He stole my father's place. He and his friends and—," Brett couldn't say more. Thinking of Allie's betrayal was too much.

Gideon looked at him somewhat expectantly, but Brett was suddenly too tired to talk.

"Thank you for helping me," he finally offered. "I hope I don't bring trouble down on you."

"Your father and mother were friends to us when no one else was. This Wyoming is a savage place, wild, and filled with hard people. Your father sold us a few of his steers when we needed them. This is the least we could do."

"Still, I don't want to be trouble."

"You won't be. No one will even know you're here. We don't deal with outsiders often and who's going to find you in here?" Gideon gestured to the room.

Brett guessed it was a spare bedroom in Sweeney's house. The walls were painted white and the furniture, a small table and chair, while well built, were plain and unadorned. Light came in from the only window and all he could see outside was a few high wispy clouds.

A knock came from the door and a man a few years older than Gideon entered.

"Brett, this is Doctor Wahlquist, he is our community physician. He's the one who saw to your wounds," Gideon said.

"Nice to finally meet you," Wahlquist offered his hand and Brett took it. The grip was firm and steady. Wahlquist studied him through a set of tiny spectacles. His hair and mustache were iron grey and his eyes so dark Brett couldn't see the irises. "Well young man, you gave us quite a scare."

"I'm going to be fine then?" Brett asked.

"I believe so. You are through the worst of it. The arm may be a little stiff. Some of the tendons were damaged. Not much I could do for those," he said.

"Will I still be able to use it?"

"Oh yes," Wahlquist snorted. "Never be quite like it was, but given time you will be fine. You are lucky infection did not set in. If it had you could have lost your right arm entirely."

"Thank you," Brett said.

"Well, I did some of the work, but in truth it was Lisa who mostly took care of you. After I removed the slugs she cleaned and dressed your wounds," Wahlquist said. He smiled at Gideon. "She did a fine job. You should be proud of her Gideon."

"Of course," he nodded. "I am proud of all my children."

"Please thank her for me," Brett said. He vaguely remembered a blonde girl, a few years younger than himself, from when he and his father drove the cattle down off the mountain. Skinny little thing who'd been all knees and elbows.

"You can thank her yourself. But you need to rest now. We will leave you to it," Wahlquist said.

"I'll ask Lisa to bring you something to eat in a moment," Gideon said.

He and Gideon left, closing the door behind them.

Brett lay awake, thoughts racing, unable to take their advice and rest. There was too much that needed doing. He had to find a way to move Kip Lane off the ranch. He tried to rise. He needed to speak to Sheriff Payson down in Pryor. His arms trembled like a newborn calf as he hoisted himself up. The right one hurt like the devil.

The door opened and a girl carrying a steaming bowl entered.

"Well now. I don't think Doctor Wahlquist will appreciate you tearing open all the stitches he sewed in you," she said.

Brett gritted his teeth with the pain. His strength fled all at once and he sagged back into bed.

Then he looked at the girl and found for the second time since waking he couldn't speak. She was beautiful. Hair a golden blonde, with bright blue eyes, and a wide easy smile. Her cheeks held the barest hint of rosy color.

"Not so tough as you imagined," she said. She set the plate on the table and slid the chair over. "Well at least you'll be able to feed yourself."

Brett felt his cheeks flush. "I wasn't quite so well as I thought."

"Three gunshots will do that." She gave him a knowing look and Brett wasn't sure what to say. Did she think he was an outlaw? "I'm Lisa by the way. You probably don't remember me but I was with father when you brought those cows down to us a few years ago."

"I think I remember you. The skinny little girl," he said. He cringed as he heard the words. *That's not something she'll like hearing.*

"Well, glad I made an impression," she said surprising him with a grin. "I remember you riding a black horse."

"Polk, first horse my father gave me."

"Sorry to hear about your parents. They were good people," Lisa said. She changed subjects quickly. "If you lean forward I can prop you up better and you can eat. Mama made this chicken dumpling for you."

Brett strained forward and Lisa stuffed another pillow beneath him.

"There." She handed him the bowl, a spoon, and a little white napkin.

"Thank you." The soup smelled wonderful and his stomach growled for it. He started to eat but his right hand fumbled the spoon. He finally got hold of it, scooped up a dumpling, and tried raising it to his mouth. Halfway there a lance of pain shot through his elbow. He dropped the spoon and spilled it on the blanket.

"Sorry," he scowled at his hand. "My arm doesn't want to cooperate."

"That's alright," Lisa used the napkin to clean away the spill.

Brett tried again, this time with his left hand. It felt awkward. The spoon's handle didn't seem to cooperate and he missed his mouth the first try. For a long time he held that first heavenly bite in his mouth, chewing slowly, and squeezing out the flavor. It tasted perfect.

Lisa giggled when he spilled broth down over his chin. Brett was too hungry to care.

He ate until he had scraped the bowl dry.

"Doctor Wahlquist said you would be hungry like a bear in spring. He said I shouldn't give you more just yet though. Let your stomach get used to eating again first," Lisa said.

Brett frowned. He wanted to stuff himself enough to burst. It felt like he hadn't eaten in a year. Still his stomach was full and warm and suddenly he was very tired.

I need to get up. I need to get to Pryor and speak to the Sheriff.

"Go ahead and sleep," Lisa said. She tilted her head to one side. Then spoke as if she could read his thoughts. "Remember how weak you were trying to get up on your own. You won't be getting out of bed for some time yet."

Brett thought about his aching arm. He didn't want to embarrass himself again. Pryor would wait. He could ride in and speak to the Sheriff when he was well.

4

———

Two days passed before Brett was able to climb out of bed. Two more before he could dress himself. During that time Lisa cared for him, cleaned his wounds, made sure he was fed. They didn't talk often—she had other chores for her family—and sometimes one of her older sisters took her place, and Brett began feeling a sense of loss whenever she was gone.

The Sweeneys were a large family. Lisa was the youngest and there were three older sisters, Sarah, Ruth, Mary, all mirror images of each other and Jane, their mother. She also had two older brothers, Joseph and Jacob.

"Lisa doesn't sound biblical like the others," Brett said one day.

"Short for Elizabeth. She was the mother of John the Baptist," Lisa had laughed.

A week after he'd arrived Brett took his first walk around Youngston. Lisa went with him. Lady Autumn had taken back the weather; the day was mild and sunny. A line of geese honked overhead. He saw families out working, chopping wood for the long winter to come, chinking up their cabins, putting the last few jars of vegetables in their dugout cellars.

All of Youngston seemed to be up and working.

"All but me," Brett said to himself. He flexed his right hand. He'd regained a measure of the old feeling and dexterity, but his elbow was still sore especially when he tried lifting anything. His left hand seemed to get better with use, he could easily eat with it now, and routine tasks were starting to seem more natural.

"What?" Lisa asked.

"Just thinking everyone else has something to do here," Brett said.

"Should we keep going?"

"Yes, I'm tired of laying around all day. I've never gone a week without riding or checking cows or doing some kind of chores."

"Do you like living up there on the ranch by yourself?"

"It's lonesome, but you get used to it. With all your brothers and sisters I imagine it's very different than what you're used to. Everyone here has such large families." They walked past a group of four boys repairing the fence around their barn while their father looked on.

"You were an only child?" Lisa asked.

"Yes."

"I can't imagine the silence."

As they walked a number of people waved; several stopped what they were doing to talk with Lisa. Young or old everyone seemed to have a kind word for her. The boys gave Brett distant looks and the girls would usually smile and blush when Lisa introduced him. Overall the community seemed to have accepted him as the Sweeney's guest.

No doubt they remember mother and father and the beef we sold.

Though they spoke little, Brett enjoyed walking with Lisa. She seemed to enjoy it as well.

When they returned Gideon Sweeney was relaxing in a rocking chair on the porch.

"Have a seat," he said. "I've been thinking about your problem."

"I'll go help mother with dinner. Thank you Brett, for the walk," Lisa said and disappeared in the house.

"My problem getting the ranch back?" Brett asked.

"I am afraid things are worse than you imagine. Sheriff Wills will not act beyond the town of Pryor."

"Wills?" Brett hesitated "I thought Bill Payson was the Sheriff?"

"He was until last month. Payson's wife became ill and they went back east to seek better treatment. It was rather sudden. A man named Jason Wills is the new Sheriff."

"I don't know anyone named Wills."

Sweeney looked out into the distance.

"He rode in working for Davis Judd. I am not sure if he's a friend to Kip Lane, but I doubt he will go against him." Sweeney leaned back in his chair. "Two nights ago Lane killed another man down in Pryor over a card game. Apparently the other man was known as a gunfighter."

"You've heard a lot."

"Quincy Hoefman went into Pryor this morning stocking up on salt, sugar, and flour for the winter. The shooting was the talk of the town."

"Nothing about Lane stealing my ranch?"

"Well...interesting thing about that. Lane is not staying out at your ranch. An older man named Seth Nelson is. He too is a gunman riding for Davis Judd."

"Another gunfighter?" Brett's hopes sank. *Now there are two of them to contend with.* "Why would Lane take the ranch and give it to this Nelson?"

"Maybe he and Nelson are partners. Regardless Davis Judd has moved a few hundred of his cows over to your place, and Nelson seems to be watching both them and yours."

"Your friend Quincy hears an awful lot," Brett said.

"His wife is quite the gossip," Gideon smiled. "And given our position in Wyoming—how people treat us—we use that to our advantage. It always pays to listen."

To Brett the whole situation was a blur. All he knew was that he had to get his father's ranch back. He owed it to his parents. But with gunfighters involved, two of them now, and if this new Sheriff, Jason Wills, wouldn't help him then what could he do?

"What will you do now?" Gideon asked.

"I don't know. I've got to get the ranch back. It's all my parents had. It's all they ever wanted was for me to have my own place."

"Is that what you want?"

Brett hesitated. In truth, he wasn't sure what he wanted. His parents had always just assumed he would marry Allie and settle down on the ranch, and he had never considered any other options. "Yes, and I've got to find a way to run these gunfighters out. I don't know what Lane told Mr. Judd—maybe he told him he bought the ranch off me—but if I talk to him I'm sure we can sort this all out."

Gideon grimaced. "I suspect Davis Judd is actually the man behind all of this."

"What do you mean?"

"Look at it this way. It is quite convenient that a number of men who all work for Davis Judd shot you, another of his men is now living at your house, and he has driven his cattle onto your range."

"But he offered to buy me out after my father's death. I turned him down. He didn't seem angry about it."

"And now he and his men have taken what's yours," Gideon said. "While another of his men is the new Sheriff."

"I'm sure it's just a coincidence. Mr. Judd struck me as a sincere man," Brett said. Still he couldn't escape Gideon's suspicions entirely.

It does make a kind of sense. From the outside it must certainly look that way, but why offer to buy me out?

Gideon said nothing. He gave Brett a weighing look.

Brett circled back to the problem at hand. "I'm not sure there's much I can do at this point. I only know that I've got to try something."

Sweeney looked out toward the Bighorns. "This is a hard land, lad. Harder by far than the place Brigham settled us. There we had only to fight the land and not other men. I'm not sure what the future holds for us here. The people are violent. The law and its protections do not exist. Evenings like this are pleasant enough, but sometimes I wish we were back in the desert among our own kind."

———

ONE WEEK LATER, almost three weeks after he'd been shot, Brett rode out of Youngston. The Sweeneys said their goodbyes and sent their well wishes. He liked these people. They worked hard, and stayed close as a family. He would miss their noisy bustling house, and the evening walks with Lisa, talking and laughing.

More than anything he wished he could have spent more time with her.

He paused at on top of a long low ridge just east of town, and then he looked back to see Lisa standing alone on her father's porch, watching him. He waved, she returned it, and then he swung toward the mountains.

Someday I want her to visit the ranch. The quiet, the high lonesomeness of the place. She'll love it. First though I've got to take it back from Kip Lane and this new man, Seth Nelson.

His horse had been well cared for and he carried his belongings along with a few extra blankets the Sweeneys hadn't needed. He still didn't have a plan to get his father's ranch back, but he rode back up to the old mining claim to be alone and think.

On the way Brett passed several groups of Judd's cattle mixed in with his father's. Anger flared hot in his chest as he looked at them milling about on his range, eating his grass.

I have to move them off somehow.

The mining shack was just as he'd left it. He circled the place twice before approaching, riding slow and keeping to the thickest trees where he could, searching for tracks and seeing none.

Lane and his friends haven't found this place so far. Do they still think I'm dead?

Well there was very little to draw them up this way. The cattle preferred the better grasses that grew to the south or lower down.

Brett thought about his escape. Maybe Lane and his men thought the corral fence had fallen on its own and his mare had just wandered out, or maybe they were just to lazy to care. *My good luck either way and I'll take it.*

With only a little fire for comfort, he spent the night in the shack and was no closer to solving his problem. Over the next few days he fixed some of the leaks around the windows and patched holes in the walls. He found several loose boards that rattled in the wind and nailed them back down in place. He cleared the fallen tree off the corral fence, replaced the broken railing with one he trimmed out of a short lodgepole pine, and turned his mare loose inside.

There was a clearing not far away and he found an old sickle to cut a few bundles of hay. Of fallen wood there was plenty, and Brett set about with an axe, splitting it into chunks small enough to feed the little stove.

He explored the area some, slaughtered one of his yearling steers, and hung it in the mineshaft where it was cooler. The elk were drifting down from the high places. He had his old single-shot hunting rifle, but decided not to risk a shot unless he had to. In the mountains the sound of a gunshot would carry far. He did not want to be discovered; Kip Lane could be anywhere.

At night Brett tried drawing his father's Colt. But try as he might he never seemed to improve. He went through the motions slowly and everything went fine, and then when he tried drawing faster, he either fumbled the grip or dropped the Colt completely. He just couldn't get the hang of it.

Frustrated one night, he switched the holster around and tried with his left hand. It felt cumbersome and strange, but the draw was smooth, and his left arm felt both strong and swift. He kept practicing with the left until he could draw and point quickly, then he would stop and check to make sure his aim was correct. Whenever he went out during the day, either to explore or gather more hay for the mare, he kept drawing the Colt left-handed. He drew on rabbits or birds as he flushed them from cover. He practiced at targets across his body, straight ahead, and even behind. He had to be ready for trouble from any direction.

He got better. He could feel it in his movements. Drawing the gun felt more natural and far quicker too. Still he was no gunfighter. He knew practicing his draw wasn't the same as facing a man down and killing him. Kip Lane had killed lots of men and likely this other fellow, Seth Nelson, had as well.

Shooting near the cabin was too great a risk, so Brett rode north and then east down into a deep cut lined with spruce where the sound wouldn't travel. He lined up pinecones and empty cans on a fallen log. He shot at them from the draw and sometimes with the Colt up at eye level. He started out missing his targets often, but slowly improved until he could move further back and repeat the process.

He found an old miner's lamp and candles then spent a day searching his way along through the abandoned mine. He didn't see any sign of gold; he wasn't sure he would know what to look for.

The third week in the cabin it rained. A hard high mountain downpour of thunder and lightning and drops so large they stung. The ceiling leaked in a dozen places and the next morning Brett carved bits of wood into wedges and hammered them into the larger holes on the inside, then he laid down a new layer of sod over the roof.

Should stop the leaks and keep the place a little warmer.

Winter was well on its way. There was frost on the windows every morning now. The grass had died back into tufts of brown. Brett grew frustrated. So much time had passed and he was no closer to solving his problems.

A month after he'd left Sweeney's he decided to see about his father's cabin.

Keeping to the trees, he made his way down to the foothills and tied up his horse in a grove of evergreens just upslope from the cabin. Then he snuck down closer. He had a mind to search the place for more grub if there wasn't anyone there.

A brush-covered ridge ran north and south between the house and the higher meadows. A good place to watch the cabin from. He found a thick clump of sage and other brush and crawled beneath it where he could peer down toward the barn and corrals.

A trace of white smoke rose from the house's chimney. There were several horses in the corral he didn't recognize, and somehow they'd gotten his father's prize stallion Cimarron in there.

How'd they ever manage to catch him?

Cimarron only responded to Brett or his father. Anyone else who came near he either ignored completely or, if they were unlucky, he might try to bite or kick. Years back a rustler tried to take the big stallion from the south pasture and Cimarron had almost killed him. After that word spread and no one tried stealing him again.

After an hour of watching, a pair of cowboys came out of the house. They caught up their horses and then headed off toward the south.

Riding for Pryor most likely, Brett decided.

He waited another half hour. He started to rise when he heard a horse off to his left, and eased back down as three men rode over the ridge just a few yards from where he lay hidden.

Two of the men he recognized instantly. Kip Lane and Davis Judd. The third was someone he hadn't seen before. The man was older than Lane, maybe a few years younger than Davis Judd. He had sandy shoulder-length hair and a strong unshaven jaw. The skin around his green eyes stood out with crow's feet.

They stopped just over the ridge while Davis lit a cigar.

"I tell you this is a fine, fine place," he said.

"It fits in well with your other ranch," the third man said.

"Yes, Hollande says we should be able to run almost three thousand head on what I've got now."

"You should have let me kill that ranch kid earlier," Lane said. "I could have done it weeks ago."

"No," Davis shook his head. "You've got to plan ahead Kip. Find out if he has any relatives who might inherit, find out if he has any friends in the community who could be a problem. Besides it took that long to get Jason into the Sheriff's job. Everything had to be set in place first."

"Look it's all well and good that we have this now, but when are we going to root out those damned Mormons?" Lane said.

"All in good time boy," Davis said around his cigar. "Have a little patience. Things are in motion. I've got to meet with the Governor next month, and then he and I will discuss those squatters over in

Youngston. This is cattle country and he knows it. There's no room for that crazy religion of theirs."

"And I'll be the one to get rid of them?" Lane said.

"Of course, I don't think Seth here has any interest in that sort of thing," Davis answered. He looked expectantly at the older gunman.

The third man gave Lane a disgusted look. "I told you I'm done. No more shooting for me. I've seen too much of it. I'm getting out while my guts are still on the inside," he said.

Seth...this has to be Seth Nelson then. The other gunfighter. The one staying at the ranch.

"No getting out for me," Kip grinned, "I'll never be beat."

"Everyone gets beat sooner or later," Seth sighed. "There's always some smug youngster wanting to prove himself and eventually one catches you on an off night or when you're drunk or hungover and then that's it."

"Not me. It won't happen to me." Lane's face took on a dark intensity.

"Boys, out here men are becoming kings," Davis said. "Men with land and cattle and money. A year from now I'm going to be the biggest rancher in Wyoming. The King of all kings. I already own a Sheriff and soon I'll own the Governor."

"You aren't worried some of these homesteaders will band together against you?" Seth asked.

"The Cattleman's Association runs this state. I'll be meeting with them once I've consolidated my holdings. It seems they are already eager to have me among their number, but I want to come in from a position of real strength. I've got two thousand cows up here now and next year we'll double that. In two years this will be the largest ranch in the state, maybe even the entire west."

The three men started off toward the house and Brett watched after them. He fought back the urge to rise and start shooting. Three against one and with two of them gunfighters, he'd never succeed.

Gideon had been right.

Kip Lane didn't shoot me over Allie or to take the ranch for himself. Davis Judd planned all this. He's the man behind it.

5

After they'd gone Brett waited well over an hour before finally sneaking back to his horse. He was angry. Angry about Kip Lane...angry about Allie, angry about Davis Judd, angry about all of it. He rode without any real direction, making his way south and then a little east to skirt wide around Pryor.

Like a grey phantom, he passed among open meadows and stately trees, aspen and pine and fir. He followed an old mountain goat trail up along the craggy shoulder of the mountain.

The day wore on into late afternoon and suddenly he pulled up short on a rocky outcrop and stopped. He took a big breath and the air was clear and searing cold. He was a good many miles south of Pryor now, fifteen more at least from his own ranch, almost due west of Cloud Peak. Towering above the other peaks, the huge gray mountain looked like the flagship of some great proud navy.

Just west of him lay the old Dugan place, now Davis Judd's home. Brett rode down toward the ranch house. Among the area's original settlers, the Dugan's had built their sprawling log cabin at the edge of a wide grassy meadow where they had a view of the setting sun.

Adam and Joan Dugan had been good people, honest, hard-working, respected by all. They'd founded the town of Pryor with a trading post back when there was nothing around but wild Indians and shaggy mountain men. Two years later other settlers wandered into the area and Pryor began to grow. Then after twelve years in town, Adam announced they were selling the store and moving out to their ranch. Everyone within thirty miles turned out to help them during the building of their home. Brett's father had done the cabin's slate shingles. He'd been proud of his work and Mrs. Dugan never missed a chance to brag on that roof every time she saw him.

There were a few horses in the corral when he arrived, none saddled, and there weren't any tied in front of either the bunkhouse or the main house.

Brett slipped the thong off the Colt and rode up to the big cabin without hesitating.

He swung down, climbed up on the porch, and then slammed the front door open like he owned the place. Inside he heard a curse followed by a heavy clang.

The Colt was in his left hand before he realized he'd drawn. He turned and pointed it in the direction of the noise. To his left was a closed door. Brett's spurs jangled faintly as he moved toward it. He opened it quickly and leveled the pistol.

A Mexican in a white apron stood there holding a pan of steaming biscuits in both hands. A trace of flour lay scattered on the floor. His face was drained of color. "Ohh, thank god," he said with only a hint of an accent. "I was afraid you were an Indian—come to claim my hair—the way the door banged open."

He set the pan on the table and wiped at his hands with the apron. "I was so frightened I dropped the biscuits. If you'll wait a bit, these will cool and you're welcome to a few."

That was the way of the west; out here the stranger you fed one day might save you from Indians or a grizzly bear or help you through a blizzard. Food was not what was on Brett's mind though. He gestured with the Colt.

"Keep your hands out where I can see them."

The cook's eyes widened when he noticed the pistol for the first time. "Sí. Yes."

"Is there anyone else around? And don't bother lying to me."

"No...No..." the cook stammered. He shook his head slightly; sweat began beading up on his face. "The others...they rode out with Mr. Judd this morning."

"Go on and open up that closet. Then step back against the far wall," Brett pointed with the pistol.

"Sí, don't shoot me señor," the cook nodded.

Brett moved up to the closet and looked inside. It was lined with shelves of canned goods, sacks of flour, sugar and salt. A smoked ham hung on a hook at the back.

"Take an empty sack and fill it up with cans," Brett said. "Then take another and put that ham in it. Pile them up over there along with a sack each of salt and sugar."

The cook did as Brett ordered.

"Now put a sack of flour on the table here and then move on into that closet."

Once the man did as he'd instructed, Brett moved to the door and closed it behind the cook. There was a latch near the top and he fastened it. With the old cook trapped, he holstered the Colt. Then he picked up the first sack, carried it out, and left it near his horse. He put the second sack and all the rest of the food out beside it. He caught up a little bay horse from the corral and found a blanket and halter that fit. He loaded the food on the bay and left both horses tied loosely to the porch.

Then he moved through the house, searching room by room. One of the bedrooms had been turned into an office and he found a strongbox on a writing desk inside. It was locked, no key to be found, but he'd expected that and smashed it open with a farrier's hammer he'd taken from the barn earlier.

There was a little over a thousand dollars inside, far less than his ranch was worth, but he stuffed it into his saddlebags.

Maybe I can hire a gunfighter of my own. Someone to take on Davis Judd's men.

He went back to the kitchen and let the cook out of the closet.

The man clenched his apron in his hands. There were tears on his flour-stained cheeks.

"No. No please," he shook his head. "I won't tell anyone you were here. I don't even know you. There's no need—"

"Stop, I'm not going to kill you," Brett said. "But you can't stay here, it's going go get almighty warm in a few minutes. March ahead of me and don't get any ideas or I will shoot you."

He put the Colt's barrel in the cook's back, took one of the oil lanterns off the wall, and smashed it against one wall; he did the same with another in the main room. Then he struck a match and threw it on the spilled oil. The flames spread quickly, lapping across the floor and climbing the wall like a freed beast. He hurried outside.

In moments the house was well aflame.

For a moment, Brett stood next to the cook and watched the great house burn. He swung up into the saddle.

"If I were you I'd head for Pryor. Davis might think you did all this," Brett said.

"He is a vicious man," the cook said. "He will kill you for this."

"He already did. You tell them the ghost of Brett Rawlins came by for a visit."

Brett took both horses and started for the dark trail along the Bighorns again. As before he stopped on the overlook. The sky was dark, but he could see Davis Judd's house easily enough. Flames rose high in the night, dancing and weaving in consuming delight. With its supports weakened, the roof crashed down and a whirling wind of glowing sparks swirled out in all directions.

"Sorry father," Brett said. "I know you were awful proud of that slate roof."

———

BRETT SLEPT underneath the sweeping boughs of a huge lodgepole pine that night. He made no fire, from his height on the mountain a stray light could be seen for miles and smoke from a campfire had a way of traveling.

He ate a pair of the cook's biscuits and a few chunks torn from the ham. It was the best meal he'd had since leaving Sweeney's almost a month ago.

That Mexican knew how to cook. I hope he made it into Pryor.

The next day Brett wound his way higher into the Bighorn wilderness. He picked his way across a number of rockslides and followed an icy stream for a half-mile to mask his trail. He left the water at a moose crossing. A place well-used where the big animals would quickly erase his tracks.

There was a cave he knew about, almost due east of the ranch, a place remote and very high up.

Brett found the place easy enough, more than once he'd stayed the night here whenever he hunted among the peaks. He made a good deal of noise when he drew close to the cave's mouth—no need startling a cranky bear or mountain lion—thankfully the cave was empty.

Two weeks he stayed up there, eating Davis Judd's food, keeping warm enough with a little cooking fire in the evenings. He journeyed out on occasion; he saw Judd riders often. A hulking man, usually riding a tall lineback dun, barked orders at the other cowboys. They didn't seem to be looking for him, mainly they were just pushing even more of Judd's cattle onto his range.

After a time, when the weather had grown too cold near the peaks, he moved down back into the mining shack again. He spent the long winter months in the shack, chopping wood—the little stove's appetite was endless, practicing with the Colt, or thinking about what he might do next. The short chilly days and long frozen nights were dull and gray and lifeless.

Drawing the pistol left-handed was natural now. His wounds were recovered and—though his right hand remained a little clumsy—his back and shoulder felt fine. More than fine actually, the unending axe work and food put weight on him, filling out his arms and chest with heavy slabs of muscle. One morning he put on his father's jacket and found it was no longer loose in the shoulders.

He visited the Sweeney's a few times. He spent as much time as he could with Lisa. Her sunny disposition was a great relief after his long periods of hibernation. They went riding a time or two, but mostly they stayed near the little village.

With Judd's money he bought supplies from Gideon. He killed a beef of Judd's whenever he needed it, but ran short on salt, flour, sugar and other items regularly. The Sweeneys kept him caught up on the latest news. Kip Lane killed another man down in Worland and there were rumors of two more. Davis Judd bought out another rancher south of the Dugan place; no one seemed to know the former owner's name. Of the second gunfighter, Seth Nelson, he heard nothing.

A couple of evenings he slipped down close to his father's house where he would see Nelson just sitting on the porch smoking a cigar or having a shot of whiskey and enjoying the evening quiet.

Seth Nelson made being a gunman seem boring.

The older man didn't look much like a gunfighter. He was drawn and grizzled with tired eyes and shaggy brown hair, and he certainly didn't act like act like a gunfighter. Brett thought he'd be down in town with the others every evening, having a drink and chasing a saloon girl or two. Nelson seemed content just to smoke his cigar and sit rocking in his chair. Now and then he'd walk over to the corral to feed Cimarron a carrot or half an apple and give the horse a scratch under his neck.

Watching Nelson with the big red stallion stirred a deep sense of anger in Brett. Cimarron was his father's horse, his pride and joy. This gunfighter had no right to him.

Winter finally turned into spring and the creeks swelled with the melting runoff. A sheepherder pushed his flock along the mountain's shoulder and Brett swapped a tanned cowskin for some fresh mutton.

Tired of being trapped in the shack, Brett crossed over the mountains into the Tongue River country. Sheridan lay a few miles to the east and south and suddenly he wanted a meal he hadn't cooked himself.

Sheridan had started a few years before Pryor and was quite a bit bigger, the last gateway before the Rockies, as some called it. Mostly it was a cowtown, some mining, and a bit of trade coming from Billings down to Laramie or Denver. In the summer a number of cattle buyers would drift into town and they'd put together herds for the long drive to the railhead down in Cheyenne.

There had been talk of a rail line at one point, but so far it was only empty talk.

He stopped in at the Lucky Mary saloon. Save for the bartender, the place was empty when he walked in. The bartender himself was a greasy man with slicked back hair and a high, wide forehead. He had a rag in one hand and was rubbing down the bar for all he was worth.

"Slow today?" Brett asked.

"Most days," the man answered without looking. "Evenings aren't too bad."

"Anything to eat?"

"Yeah, I'll ask the cook. He usually puts extra on. Thinks he's still working a cattle drive and there's a dozen hungry cowhands to feed." The bartender looked up and studied him for the first time. He glanced at Brett's worn-out clothes and the down-at-heel boots. He gave Brett a dubious look, "It's two bits."

Brett flipped one of Judd's silver dollars out on the table. "Anywhere I can take a bath, maybe a shave, and some new clothes?"

"General store down the street, and the barber, Fred, is right across from there," the bartender said. He eyed the coin. "Get you anything to drink?"

Brett smiled.

After eating, picking up a few clothes, and then cleaning up at Fred the barber's place, Brett felt like a new colt. He'd kept part of his beard, but trimmed it neat and short. Studying himself in Fred's mirror he marveled at the change. Gone without a trace was the boyish face he remembered. His face was lean now, dark and hardened by work, and he had grown another inch or two.

I'm taller now than father was.

In his features he could see much of his father mixed with hints of his mother as well, but he would have outweighed Jim Rawlins by a good thirty pounds. Mostly across the shoulders and chest. He'd come a long way since last spring. He certainly wasn't a boy anymore. He put the extra clothes, along with his old gear and some supplies, on the little bay packhorse.

He returned to the bar and decided to have another meal before heading out. There was a hotel across the street though, and he was sorely tempted at the thought of sleeping a night in a real bed.

"Anything would be better than the hard floor of that damned shack," he muttered. He tied up his horses in front of the saloon and went inside.

Maybe if the food's good I'll stay a night.

There were a dozen men inside, mostly cowboys. The greasy man was still at the bar when he returned. "Help you sir," he said.

"Beer and a plate of grub," Brett said.

The bartender gave him a strange look. "Were you in here earlier?"

Brett flipped another silver dollar on the bar. "I was."

"Thought I recognized the voice," he smiled.

There was an empty table near the back and Brett took it. The cowboys were talking about the Johnson County War—Sheridan wasn't far from it. The Wyoming Cattleman's Association had declared war on the smaller outfits and farmers; there had already been several shootings. So far the Governor hadn't intervened, rumor was he approved of the Association's actions.

Brett only half-listened. He had enough problems of his own.

The food was good. Not great, but he wasn't about to complain. More cowboys came in, and one of them drew his attention. The newcomer was a loudmouth, laughing and carrying on at the bar, and though he spoke with a drawling southern accent, Brett was sure he'd seen him before.

The loudmouth bought a few drinks; he seemed friendly with several men, but they mostly ignored him.

Then the cowboy went outside for a few minutes and soon returned. He stood at the door and looked over the room before calling out, "Who's riding that little bay outside?"

Brett knew then where he'd seen the man before. He rode for

Davis Judd. The loudmouth had recognized the bay, likely by its brand, and although he might not know Brett was the man who'd burned down Judd's house, he would certainly know that the horse didn't belong to him.

Brett slipped his hand under the table to check the thong on the Colt. He'd bought a new holster in the store but had only drawn the gun from it a few times, when the clerk wasn't looking. No need in showing anyone whether he was fast or not.

Truthfully, Brett didn't know himself. He'd never even seen a real gunfight.

"I said who's riding that Bay outside? The one with the 9O brand?" He'd grown louder now. The place was quiet. Every man in there glanced from one to another. The locals knew each other well enough to sort out what horses they rode.

It won't be long before they notice me. Maybe they'll pass me over.

Brett kept eating. He kept his eyes on his plate and his left hand near his leg, down beside his father's Colt. The cowboys began shuffling around uncomfortably.

The room grew even more silent and he slanted his eyes up. Everyone was looking at him now.

The loudmouth cowboy stepped forward. "Deaf are you?"

Brett said nothing. His mind raced, trying to find a way out. There had to be something. Some explanation for the horse.

The loudmouth took a step forward. "Mister, no one has seen that horse in quite some time. In fact no one's seen it since my boss, Davis Judd, had his house burned down by some no good snake."

The cowboy shifted his legs apart and hooked his thumbs behind his belt buckle.

"Only a damned coward would burn down a man's house while he was away," he said.

Brett just sat. It struck him that there was something even more familiar about the man.

Something about his voice.

It clicked then. This was one of the Kip Lane's friends. One of the men who'd ambushed him and left him for dead in the crevasse. The one who'd spoken about Allie. Deep in Brett's chest anger flared, hot and bright. He took the last bite then wiped his mouth with the napkin. His hat lay beside him and he scooped it up and put it on. Then he stared up at the loudmouth.

"Only a pack of cowards would ride out after a man and shoot him in the back three against one." Brett's voice was hard. And despite the fire in his chest it was icy cold. It surprised him. "Especially while they had someone hold his arms down where he couldn't fight back."

The loudmouth paused. For a second he looked confused. His mouth dropped open in surprise.

"No one knew about that. No one but us. No one but..." the cowboy squinted hard at Brett. He took a step back. His hand fell near his gun. "No. You're dead. You're a damned ghost. You fell into that hole after we killed you."

"But I'm not dead. I'm sitting right here. I've finished my meal and now I'm going to stand up and kill you." Brett meant it. The loudmouth might be faster; he might be more accurate. He almost certainly had more experience. But Brett suddenly knew he'd kill him.

I've never even shot at a man. But it won't matter. He may get me, but no matter what happens, whether he kills me or not, I'm putting lead in him.

Brett stood and the loudmouth moved back another half-step. His hand inched lower. Cowboys behind him scrambled to one side or the other out of Brett's line of fire.

"Kill you now, you damned ghost." The loudmouth twitched. His hand moved down and suddenly Brett's Colt was out spewing flame and lead.

Three times, he fired. Three times, the loudmouth's body jerked. And then he fell dead.

"By Gawd, that was fast," one of the cowboys let out after a long whistle.

"Self-defense. The dead fellow drew first," another said.

Brett holstered his Colt without a word and stepped outside. He stopped just beyond the swinging saloon doors, leaned down, and threw up. His chest felt tight like he'd been wrapped in bands of iron. He held out his hands and they trembled.

Before anyone could see, he wiped his mouth, climbed onto his horse, and rode for the Bighorns.

6

Brett rode late into the night. He camped on the eastern slope of the mountains well shy of the windswept pass. The moon rose, bright and clear, and lit the flat expanse of long grassy plains below.

For several hours, he sat up watching his campfire. His hands continued to shake. He tried to calm them, but they wouldn't still. He'd killed a man. Over and over he replayed what happened in his mind. He needed a distraction, but the only thing he could think to do was practice drawing his Colt. Something he never wanted to do again.

Finally, sometime near midnight he calmed. *I'm being foolish. It was him or me. He would have killed me; hell he already tried once before.*

He took out his Colt and studied it in the firelight. *Such a quick thing to end a man's life.* A scant few seconds cutting short a lifetime. He replaced the three spent cartridges and shoved the pistol back into the holster. Running out of town had probably been a mistake. No doubt the town Marshal would have questions, still the shooting was justified. Everyone at the bar knew he'd been called out. They all knew the Judd man drew first.

The law is the least of my worries. I've still got Seth Nelson, Kip Lane, and Davis Judd to worry about.

He knew he could not afford to be squeamish over the loud-mouth's death. There might be more shooting in the days ahead. More killing. Men had tried to kill him and they would again. Whenever they did, he could not afford to hesitate. To survive he would have to kill them first. He had to be strong. He had to harden himself for what was sure to come.

The first bright rays of dawn found him near the high pass. The snow here still lay in deep drifts, but there had been enough travelers to clear away a decent trail. He paused in the pass long enough to take in the view. The day was clear and he could see for miles. The Bighorn River wound along down below like a blue string ever making its way north to join up with the Yellowstone.

Down off the pass, he decided to try and find the Great Medicine Wheel. He'd heard about the wheel years ago from an old trapper who stopped by the ranch. Almost nothing was known of it. Who'd built it and for what purpose? According to the trapper, the Cheyenne and Shoshone claimed only that it was sacred to all tribes. The Crow were supposed to know more, but it was hard to get any Indian to even speak of the place.

After an hour of searching, he broke into a clearing and noticed a number of rocks all neatly arranged in a long gently-sweeping curve. His eyes followed the curve's path to a line of intersecting rocks.

He climbed down off his horse and walked along the line. More lines ran on either side and soon they all met in a mound of loose stone piled up in the center. Brett picked up one of the stones and ran his fingers over it.

Smooth and round. From the river then, but the Bighorn is still miles away. Whoever built this must have hauled these all the way up from below. Why not use the rough local stone?

There were certainly plenty laying scattered all around. He looked all around over the huge Wheel in its entirely.

How old must this be? And how much work someone put into it.

Brett placed the smooth rock back on the pile just as it had been. He started back across the Wheel when he noticed a shadowy figure standing out away from the trees.

"Sorry," Brett said. "Didn't see you there."

"Most people don't," the figure's voice was low and flat.

"Do you know anything about the Wheel? How old do you think it is?"

The figure stepped forward into the light. He wore buckskins—frayed at the edges to help shed water—a string of white and black beads mixed with polished animal teeth around his neck, and a pair of eagle feathers tied up in his hair.

On instinct Brett's hand started for the Colt.

The Indian smiled at him. "If I intended to kill you it would have been easy enough when you were lost in thought. And I know only a little about the Wheel."

He turned his attention to the central mound. "It is old of course, built long before my people came to this land. Some of our stories tell that the ancient ones built it before journeying west into the setting sun and the great misty lands beyond. Others say it was the little people who dwell among the high quiet places to celebrate the fullness of summer."

"You are Cheyenne?" Brett asked.

"Crow," the Indian said. "I am Red Elk."

"I've never met a Crow. A few Cheyenne visited Pryor now and then."

"We stay on the lands your Great White Chief set aside for us. We honor the treaty."

"Yet you are here?" Brett asked.

"Few enough of my tribe even remember the Wheel is here. Our ways are dying," Red Elk's gaze moved into the distance. "Just as the ways of the ancients did."

"You came to see the Wheel then? It is sacred to your people?"

"It is sacred to all tribes. It is a place of peace among all. To keep from offending the Spirits we do not make war here. I came to speak with them. Seeking their wisdom."

"I understand. I will leave you to it," Brett said. He led his horse back toward the trail.

Without speaking further, the Indian watched him go.

Brett swung up into the saddle and started down the long trail. He turned off well before Pryor swinging north and then west to circle through the ranch. He left his supplies in the mining shack, along with the packhorse, and then went on down to Youngston.

A week had passed since he'd been there last and he wanted to see Lisa.

It was late when he arrived at the Sweeney's place. Jane Sweeney, Lisa's mother, met him at the door.

"Mr. Rawlins, do come in. It's been awhile since we've seen you."

"Yes ma'am. Too long."

"We were just settling down for supper and I'm sure Gideon will want you to join us," she said. Jane Sweeney resembled her daughter. The same happy eyes and golden blonde hair with only a trace of gray along the strands.

"Thank you Mrs. Sweeney. That's very kind. But you don't have to call me Mr. Rawlins." She was old enough to be his mother.

"You look very well Brett," she said and looked over his new clothes. "How have you been?"

"Thank you," Brett blushed. "I've been good enough. And yourselves?"

"I'll let Gideon fill you in," she said and then led the way into the dining room where the family was gathered around their meal.

Gideon rose and smiled when he saw him.

"Brett, good to see you boy. It has been far too long. Please have a seat," he gestured to an empty chair between himself and Lisa, and for a moment Brett thought Lisa's cheeks colored.

The family ate in relative silence, only exchanging a few pleasantries, mostly talking about the weather or range conditions or planting times, and when they were done he and Mr. Sweeney retired to the quiet of the porch.

"It's good to see you sir. Things are well here in Youngston?" Brett said.

"Actually..." Gideon paused. "Things are quite poor at the moment. Davis Judd's men have been stirring up trouble."

"Trouble?"

"There have been some...incidents. Last week one of our men went to Pryor for supplies and was stopped on the trail. They roughed him up and told him no one in Pryor would sell to us anymore."

"Is it true?"

"Who knows," Gideon shrugged. "Davis Judd has opened a bank in Pryor and he's loaned money to the stores, most of them were struggling to survive, and no doubt each now owe him a great sum. After buying out Ned Winter, he also has the only freight service. He could easily ruin anyone willing to do business with us."

"What does he have against you? This isn't on my account?"

"No," Gideon shook his head. "I don't think they even know you're alive. Not for certain at least. There were a few rumors though..."

"Rumors?"

"Rumors that you burned down Judd's ranch house. Rumors that he had horses missing and over a thousand dollars from a strongbox. A Mexican cook was telling the tale, but no one really believed him."

Gideon looked at him expectantly.

"All true I'm afraid," Brett hung his head. He could feel Sweeney's disapproval. "You were right about Davis Judd. I came across he and some of his men and heard them talking about what they'd done to steal my father's place. So I rode over to his house, knowing he and most of his hands weren't there, and I found his strongbox along with some food. There wasn't enough money to pay for my father's ranch and cattle of course. And before I left I set fire to his house."

Brett paused and silence hung between them.

"This is a bad business Brett, all of it. Dangerous."

"I was just so angry at all of it. I felt powerless. I'm no gunfighter. I wanted to hurt him like he deserved."

"I understand," Gideon said. "But this isn't the way. You can't meet violence with violence. In time Wyoming will change. It's changing already. Men like Davis Judd have seen their day. Soon enough he will come to his just rewards."

There was a quiet strength in his words. A resolve that Brett envied.

I don't know if I agree about Davis though. The man certainly seemed to be having his way with things.

"What am I to do in the meantime? The law won't help me, Davis owns the new Sheriff, you said so yourself."

"Well, you might try writing to the Governor."

"The Governor is friends with the Cattle Association. I heard the stories over in Sheridan. Down in the Powder River country they are killing settlers and driving them off their land. He won't help." Brett decided to change the subject. "What are you going to do without the supplies from Pryor?"

"I've written the Governor myself. In the short term we'll be able to get what we need from Billings."

"The trip is longer. Two days at least."

"Yes," Gideon said. "There will be hardship, but we've known such before. Any you? What will you do Brett?"

"I don't know. The law won't help me and neither will the Governor. I'll find my own way to get my father's land back."

For a long time neither spoke. An owl hooted from his perch atop the barn and in the distance coyotes sang their evening chorus.

"You could live among us," Gideon said. "We could use a bright young man who knows cattle and the land like you do. I know Lisa would like that."

"I don't know. As you heard, I've done some pretty bad things." Purposefully, Brett didn't tell him about the shooting back in Sheridan. These were gentle folk and he valued their friendship.

"Well, think it over," Gideon said. "No matter what you've done the door is always open. Forgiveness has no limit."

———

ON THE COLD ride back toward the mine Brett considered Gideon's offer. Could he give up his father's dreams and move into Youngston? He'd never have to draw his Colt again. He could settle down into a quiet life of farming in the little Mormon community.

Mother would have wanted that for me, a life of peace without the need for violence, but father? Brett knew the answer. His father wanted him to have the ranch and carry on his legacy.

The thought of living down in Youngston was tempting though. He could see Lisa every day.

Brett banished these thoughts. None of it was practical of course. In fact, it was just a dangerous dream. He couldn't hide among the Mormons forever. Once Davis Judd learned he was alive, Kip Lane would be sent for him.

He had a sudden urge to ride into Pryor. It had been months since he'd seen the town and he wanted to look over Judd's bank and freight office. It was already dark enough to slip into town unnoticed. With his new clothes and beard no one would recognize him; beyond just the clothes the long months of chopping wood had packed another twenty pounds of muscle onto his chest and shoulders. The loudmouth over in Sheridan hadn't known him until Brett had practically told him. Brett Rawlins had emerged from the long winter a changed man.

No, more like a grown man instead of a boy.

Now he had a man's work ahead of him. He had to figure out how to defeat a pair of gunslingers, their boss, along with his other men, and take his father's ranch back. The task seemed impossible.

How can I fight all of them? The odds were just too great. In all the months since he'd been shot, the answer was no closer.

Pryor consisted of just a few sleepy streets. The road from Youngston widened to become Main Street, passed through town, and then swung south again toward Worland. There were four cross streets, but all the businesses were lined up on Main, shoulder-to-shoulder like soldiers standing at attention. There were trees everywhere, aspen and cottonwood and the occasional evergreen. With the backdrop of the rising Bighorns and the shallow river coursing through the heart of town, Pryor was beautiful.

Brett rode slowly and the moon was rising when he made the edge of town. The General Store looked the same, as did the town's only hotel. He stopped and got a room under the name Stanton.

Then he stabled his horse and headed down the boardwalk along Main.

Pryor had two saloons, though both had changed names so many times he didn't bother keeping track. They sat on opposite sides of Main Street. Light poured from the windows in each and inside men were laughing.

A cowboy stepped out from the nearer of the two for a smoke. He struck a match, cupped his hands close, and then leaned against one of the wooden columns. Finally, he spotted Brett. "Evening," he said.

"Evening," Brett answered. "The freight company at the edge of town?"

"Yeah, ahead and to your left. You might find Jasper there. He keeps late hours. Otherwise he'll be back in the morning."

"Thanks," Brett tipped his hat.

He passed by the saloons and then the Sheriff's office. There was a poster nailed to one of the posts, and he stopped to read it.

WANTED

Dead or Alive

Patrick 'Curly Red' Flanagan

For burning the 9O Ranch house and theft of ranch
property.

$400.00

Under his breath, Brett laughed. He'd told the cook he was the ghost of Brett Rawlins, but evidently they didn't believe the old Mexican.

He kept walking up the street just as the cowboy said. Along the way he passed by a new single-story building with a painted sign hanging out front. Pryor National Bank. The place couldn't have been a month old; Brett could still smell sawdust and fresh paint.

This must be Judd's. The man was setting deep roots in Pryor just as Gideon had warned.

A little further up the street Judd's other new venture, the freight office, slept dark and deserted.

Jasper must have had better things to do this evening.

Keeping to the shadows, Brett circled the building. There were two doors, one in the front, another larger one for loading and unloading freight in the rear. The front was well lit both from the open street and from a window in one of the saloons.

He approached the shadowed backdoor. To his surprise, there was no lock. The big door looked like it was held on the inside with only a simple latch. Brett drew his knife and slid it between the door and frame then lifted the latch until it fell free.

Colt drawn, he slipped inside. The warehouse's interior was divided into rows, each filled with stacks of boxes, bags, crates, and a great number of wooden barrels. He checked one of the crates. Ammunition. Another contained half a dozen new repeating rifles. He pocketed a couple boxes of rounds and picked up one of the rifles.

His old single-shot hunting rifle was back in the mine shack where he'd left it, and this would be a much better weapon.

Moving along to the back of the room he found an iron cage. Empty, the cage was easily five foot deep, floor to ceiling, and it took up the building's entire south wall.

What is this for?

If Judd wants to protect his wares then why not lock up the entire building? And why was it empty? The rifles and ammunition alone were worth a fortune.

Brett started toward the cage when there was a sound from the street outside. Horses. The rattle of a wagon. Then voices. And they were coming from the door he'd come in.

He looked for a way out. There were hiding places a plenty, but none that would conceal him for long. He noticed a trapdoor in the floorboards, just outside the cage. He lifted it open, jumped down without looking, and then eased it shut behind him.

Brett moved to the side, away from the door and nearer the building's edge. There were more crates stacked down here, all quite a bit smaller than those above; one spilled open and several round objects. Brett examined one. A plant bulb of some kind. His mother had tried planting several flowers at the ranch but none ever looked quite like this one.

Why would Davis Judd hide these beneath his freight office?

The boards creaked near the door and there were steps above along with a pair of voices.

"Damn that Jasper, I'll skin him alive leaving the door unlatched like that," one said.

"Lay off him," another man said. "He's sweet on that Wilson girl and was going to meet her tonight."

"The boss'll do worse if he finds out."

"No need for him to find out. We're here and nothing is missing. I bet Jasper ain't been gone ten minutes."

"Fine, I won't tell him, but it's on you and Jasper if the boss does find out." A long pause. Then light flooded the warehouse above. "Alright we're clear. Get em in here."

There was a sound like a number of chains rattling. They scraped and slid over the floor along with the shuffling of bare feet. Brett rose up. There was a crack in the floorboards—one large enough to see through. A shadow passed over and then he saw an Indian woman. A length of chain ran to shackles around her hands and ankles, which were all worn, raw and bloody.

"C'mon, we haven't got all night." the first man said. There was a muffled grunt from the woman and she lurched forward. For several minutes the chains kept rattling. There was at least a half-dozen women all bound together.

The cage door closed with a hard clang. A key rattled in the lock.

"Let's go get a drink. The boss'll be happy to get these to Deadwood."

"What about the crates down below?"

Brett froze. He pointed his Colt toward the trap door. If anyone decided to stick his head down through there he'd get a 45 caliber surprise.

"The opium don't go out for another couple days. The squaws are on the next load out tomorrow morning. They like them fresh out in the mines."

Brett heard the men latch the back door, and then the front door opened and closed. A set of keys jangled outside and he heard the grinding crunch of boots on gravel.

Opium. That explained the strange plant bulbs. Brett knew very little about the stuff but he'd heard it came in the bulbs of plants.

Davis Judd is selling opium and women to the miners in Deadwood. If Bill Payson were still Sheriff he could end Davis Judd on the spot. This new man though, Wills, he was one of Judd's riders. *He won't do anything.*

When their captors were gone, a few of the women started weeping. Slowly, Brett lifted the trap door. He turned around and the women all stopped weeping to stare stone-faced at him. He climbed out. One in particular, young and taller than the others with a long face and full lips, looked at him with hatefilled eyes. Unlike the others she wasn't chained at the ankle or wrist. Instead she wore a heavy iron collar around her neck and there were bruises on her hands and arms.

The door to their cage was locked and the keys were gone with the two men. He didn't like it—no one deserved to be treated like these women—but there was no way for him to free them.

Anyway I've got to get out of here before someone else shows up.

Brett turned away from them. He opened the back door again. He felt those dark, judging eyes boring into him the whole time. He used the blade of his knife to hold the latch open, closed the door back, then let the latch fall down into place.

7

B rett rose early the following day, checked out of the hotel, and made his way west into the rough country toward Heart Mountain. He had an idea that this Curly Red Flanagan might be another of the men who'd jumped him. He remembered a man with a mop of curly red hair being at his father's cabin afterwards.

To the west of Pryor people were sparse and the land was wild and rugged. There were still scattered bands of Utes and Sioux roving in the wilderness, enough to keep the settlers frightened, though they mostly kept to themselves.

He certainly wouldn't mind collecting the reward for Curly Red, especially if it meant getting a little revenge of his own.

The Shoshone River made its way westward out of Pryor and he followed the broad stretch of river bottom toward Idaho and the Yellowstone country. There were trees, cottonwood and willow, along the banks and over time the water had cut away a notch deep into the land where a man could travel well hidden down off the skyline.

There were more than a few old cabins and dugouts along the way, most well back from the river for fear of flooding. He stopped and searched several. All proved abandoned.

Such was the way of things in this country. Settlers moved in and drought or floods or heartache soon drove them out. Leaving in defeat, they took all they could carry with them of course. In the end only their empty houses remained and without care the snow and the rain soon sunk these husks back into a pile of cut logs and soggy earth.

Around noon Brett saw a hint of smoke rising a little north of the river and decided to check there.

He crested a small rise and discovered a little dugout cabin at the edge of a shallow stream. There were three horses loose in a corral nearby. Outside, braiding a new rope was a single man. But unless Curly Red meant completely bald this was not Flanagan. Brett had seen the bald man before though, herding Judd cattle on his father's ranch, and that made him an enemy.

One of Judd's riders and three horses might mean three cowboys. Could be another of the men who shot me. Maybe even Kip Lane.

Brett liked the idea of laying in wait, rifle in hand, for Lane to come out of the cabin. He couldn't imagine an easier way to settle accounts with the gunman.

He tied his horse well back off the rise out of sight in some saplings and returned with his rifle.

Crawling up on his belly, he kept low and sighted down along the rifle to the open doorway waiting to see who else might come outside. The bald man seemed pretty good at braiding the rope. Certainly he knew his business. In minutes though Brett's patience was rewarded as another man with a thick mane of fiery red hair stepped into the light. Brett studied the newcomer over his rifle's sights. Curly Red stretched in the open doorway. He gave out a huge yawn and Brett's first shot struck high, shattering the wooden doorframe right above him.

Splinters flew. Red fell back inside with a yelp and the bald man dropped the rope to dive for cover behind the corral. Brett's second and third shots were both at the bald man, each missing high again.

Brett cursed himself. "Forgot to account for the elevation," he muttered.

The barrel of a rifle appeared from one of the dugout's windows.

Brett fired twice, aiming just below the barrel, and heard the bullets hit home with a pair of solid thumps and then a scream.

Just then the bald man behind the corral broke for a grove of trees near the stream. Three more times Brett fired. His last shot spun the man around and dropped him down into the dirt.

Brett watched the fallen man for a long time, but he lay motionless. Then he fed more cartridges into his rifle.

There was more screaming from inside the dugout. Then a single shot. The screaming stopped.

Brett decided to get a better angle on the house. He stood partway up and immediately realized his mistake as a bullet whined past his ear. He instantly dropped flat and lay still. He was fairly sure the last man in the cabin couldn't see him, but he edged back behind the rise until he was certain.

With luck he'll decide he got me and come out to take a look.

Brett shifted over to his left about a hundred feet and crawled up to the rise again. At first he didn't see anything different. Then he noticed that the bald man between the cabin and the trees was gone.

I should have put another bullet in him while he was down just to be sure.

Brett no longer controlled the situation. He didn't know where his enemies were. Anything could have happened while he wasn't watching. Had the bald man made for the trees or was he back inside? And where was the third man? For all he knew he hadn't yet killed a single one. Still his position was good and he was well hidden. There was nothing to do but wait.

A half-hour passed and then he heard a loud booming shot just to the south, down close along the river.

Who could that have been? The bald man or one from inside? Suddenly his position didn't seem so good. Now they might all be out hunting him. He had no doubt they would find his horse and then himself. He needed to move.

Brett crawled back away from the cabin and quickly made his way toward his horse. *I'll head around north away from the river into the hills then circle back toward Pryor.* Just before he reached the saplings Curly Red Flanagan stepped out from behind a tree in front of him.

Red had a rifle pointed at Brett and a huge grin on his face.

Brett froze.

"Howdy," Red said. "You some kinda lawman?"

"Something like that. Wanted poster in Pryor said four hundred dollars for the man who brought you in dead or alive."

"Well," Red smirked, "I guess that's four hundred you'll never see. Funny thing is I didn't burn down no house or steal no money. I just wasn't with the others that night so they blamed it all on me."

"What about the cook?"

"Boss caught him running for Pryor babbling about a dead man and hung him," Red smirked. Then his grin slipped. "Say how'd you know about him?"

Brett only shrugged. "And the others? Your friends from the dugout."

"Dead. Like you're about to be. Adios."

Red brought the rifle up to his shoulder and Brett started for his Colt. He wouldn't make it. No one would have, but he might get lead into Red before he died.

Then a shot rang out like a cannon and Red suddenly pitched to the side. The rifle in the outlaw's hands jerked, smoke puffed from the barrel, but the bullet flew far to the right of Brett.

Brett finished his draw and fired twice, both rounds drilling Red square in the chest and slamming him to the ground. He spun on his heels, searching for whoever had fired earlier, but saw nothing.

He scanned the plains but there was nothing but the occasional small tree or clump of sagebrush. He felt exposed. Someone was watching him. Someone with a big rifle by the sound of it.

Whoever it was could have killed him at any moment, but they hadn't done so. In fact they'd saved him from a sure death. He couldn't imagine who it might be. Other than the Sweeneys, he had no friends and they were not to type to help him this way. Whoever was out there, Brett finally decided he wanted to be somewhere else.

He wasted no time loading Red across his horse then returning to the dugout. The man he must have shot through the window lay inside, two bullet wounds in his chest and another in his temple. All three horses were still in the corral and he swapped Red's body to the best of them and turned the other two loose. Then he followed the draw down to where it met the Shoshone and found the third man lying dead in a little clearing beside the river.

Brett paused to examine the body. He found where his own shot had hit the dead man in the thigh and then another right through the man's heart. Whoever killed him must have either been close or had excellent aim. The hole was larger than Brett's fist, just like the one in Curly Red.

The fallen man wore a new Colt and Brett checked it. Full. He hadn't got off a single shot.

Brett tucked the pistol into his belt for a spare, and started on for Pryor.

During the action, he'd surprised himself. After the shootout in Sheridan he'd been sick in the pit of his stomach, but this time he felt only a mild queasiness. More than anything he felt elated just to be alive.

By rights he should be dead now. Curly Red should have killed him.

Brett hadn't done anything to help himself. Like a fool, he'd made a mistake and gone crashing up to his horse without a care in the world. Curly Red almost killed him for it. Only instead of him dying some mysterious rifleman had reached out and saved him.

That wouldn't always be the case. He couldn't afford to keep making these kinds of mistakes or the next one might be his last. He couldn't rely on some hidden savior to bail him out of his own stupidity.

His thoughts turned back to his strange lack of feeling. He was almost sad at the lack of that sickness.

Is this a change for the better? Am I becoming used to the killing?

He didn't want to think of that. He did not want to become numb to killing like Kip Lane or Seth Nelson. His parents, especially his mother, would have been horrified.

————

BRETT ARRIVED BACK in Pryor in the early twilight hours heading straight for the Sheriff's office. He'd taken enough chances on being recognized and now he wanted only to collect Curly Red's reward, and then to get back to his hideout in the wilderness of the Bighorns.

Several cowboys—along with a few of the townsfolk—came out into the street to stare at him and Red as they passed through. He needn't have worried about being recognized, everyone on the street had eyes only for the dead outlaw.

The Sheriff stepped out onto his porch and met him at the office. He was a short man, with a round unshaven face and dull brown eyes.

"Jason Wills, County Sheriff," he said. He did not offer a hand.

"Stanton, and this fellow," Brett gestured to the body draped over the saddle, "is Curly Red."

"So it is, so it is," the Sheriff said. "Well there's a nice reward for him. Three hundred dollars."

"The posting says four."

"What?" Wills looked confused.

"The posting says four," Brett dipped his hat toward Red's Wanted poster.

Wills turned to squint at it. "Ahh, sure enough it does. The boys must have changed that last week when I was up Billings way."

"Must have," Brett agreed. "You want him here?"

Wills gave the dead man a distasteful look. "Nellis, you go ahead and collect Red."

A skinny man gnawing on an unlit cigar and with a bronze star pinned to his vest took the reins of Red's horse and led the dead outlaw away.

"I'll want that horse. Or you can just pay me for him. Thirty dollars sounds fair," Brett said.

"Ahh yes...of course," Wills said. "I'll have Nellis bring him back around."

"I'll just wait here if you don't mind."

The Sheriff disappeared inside and Brett pulled his hat down lower. Gossiping among themselves, the crowd soon broke up into small groups of twos and threes. Gradually, they went back to their work and—beneath the brim of his hat—Brett watched them go. He recognized less than half. There were a lot of new people in town. It had begun to feel crowded. He supposed that was true all over the west, newcomers, dreamers, fortune seekers, all coming out here to take whatever wealth they could.

Wills reappeared, his round face was flushed. He had a roll of bills in one hand. He counted out three hundreds. Brett kept his hand out.

"The reward was four hundred...plus the thirty for the horse."

"Ahh, of course." Wills added the last hundred to the pile. "Well it might be best if you just kept the horse. Can't have county money paying for horses now can we? And there's Nellis now. Nellis, why haven't you brought back this man's horse?"

"You never—" the skinny deputy stammered.

"Of course I did, I asked you to bring this man's horse back to him."

"No, you—"

"It's alright," Brett said. "Nellis was it? If you'll lead the way I'll come with you and collect him."

"Go on Nellis, go on. Show Mr. Stanton to his property," the Sheriff said.

Brett followed the deputy without comment. Nellis showed him to the horse; it stood resting one leg at a hitching rail near the undertaker's shop. Brett untied the reins, secured Red's horse behind his own, and then swung up into his own saddle.

Without speaking further, Brett started back down the street. He passed by the freight house, circling round where he could see through the now open door in the back. He climbed off his own mare and made a show of checking the hooves on Red's horse. Bent down, he glanced through the door where he could see some length of the cage inside. Empty. The shackled women were gone.

The men had said they were delivering the women to Deadwood.

They'd come in by wagon; no doubt they would have left that way as well. How else to transport a group of women in irons and chains?

They would have been on the trail before the dawn. They couldn't afford to be seen. An idea struck Brett then. If the people of Pryor knew Davis Judd was selling women—even Indian women—they'd run him out of town. What if he could somehow prove Judd was doing just that?

He would need proof. To get it he'd have to act fast.

I'll have to take one of the guards alive. Easier said than done.

Then he'd have to get them to testify against Judd. Surely they'd sell out the man to spare themselves the jail time. He cursed himself for not thinking of this last night when they were in town and everything would have been far easier.

Damn it all. If I hadn't been too busy thinking of escape and Curly Red.

Brett spurred his horse south toward Worland. The pass at Shell creek was not so steep, and the trail wide enough to admit a wagon. It was the route he would have taken.

The road skirted along the Bighorn River and the running water meandered through open grassland and lodgepole pine. He passed a few head of Judd's 9O cattle then a herd of elk feeding in a meadow.

He admired the elk, especially the tough old bulls. It took great strength to survive here, especially in the long winter months when food grew scarce and the wolves roamed about. The old bulls often carried the battle scars to prove it.

How many wars those great bulls must fight to keep what was theirs.

He saw a fire ahead and slowed the horses. It seemed early to stop, the sun was just gone, but whoever picked the spot knew his business. The road brushed up against a high sandstone cliff here and there was an overhang that kept the camp out of the worst of the weather. Directly overhead the sky was clear, but a line of towering dark clouds brewed and churned in the west.

"Hello the fire," Brett called out. He waited for a moment but no one spoke. He dismounted and approached slowly, repeating himself when he was closer. "Hello the fire. Any chance you have coffee?"

"No coffee," a strong voice said. "But you are welcome."

Brett slipped the thong off his Colt and checked to make sure it hung loose. He kept walking. There was a copper-skinned man sitting at the fire in frayed buckskins.

"We meet again," Red Elk said.

"You followed me?" Brett's hand fell to his Colt.

The Crow ignored him. "The Spirits have answered my prayers. They told me what I must do. And so I am here."

"Here to do what?" Brett relaxed a little.

"Here to help you catch the wagon," Red Elk spoke as if he didn't understand the question. He held out a hand gesturing across the fire. "Sit. Share my fire and my meal."

Nervous but deciding it was too late to do anything else, Brett tied his horses to a clump of sage and took a seat. He studied Red Elk over the flames.

The Indian was older than he'd first thought. There were flowing strands of white-gray in his hair and fine wrinkles carved along his eyes and mouth. He couldn't guess at the Crow's age.

"Thank you," Brett offered.

Red Elk gave him a stern look. "I have told you my name. I have invited you to my fire and to share my meal. It is rude not to tell me your name."

"I'm Brett Rawlins."

"Brett Rawlins," the Crow said. He looked to the darkening sky overhead as if thinking on the name. "Whites have such strange names."

"I suppose," Brett said. He gave the Crow a puzzled look. "How did you know I was chasing after a wagon?"

"The Spirits told me."

They sat in silence for a time. Brett wondered what else the Spirits might have told him. He hadn't even considered using another name; he should have. No doubt Davis Judd and the others believed he was dead. It would be best to keep it that way for now. But he didn't think the old Indian would have trouble keeping a secret. He'd bet there were a great many secrets hidden behind Red Elk's coal black eyes.

"And these Spirits...they told you to help me?"

"Yes."

"Did they also tell you where to find me?" How had the Indian known to come here? He himself hadn't even considered following the wagon until this afternoon.

"I followed you after you left the Sacred Wheel. I followed you to the hole in the mountain, the house of the desert people, and then to the place of many whites on the river and then finally to the cabin where you killed those two men."

Brett thought for a time. "Two?"

Red Elk only smiled.

"Did you kill the other one? Did you save me from Curly Red?"

Red Elk kept smiling.

If that was true, then Red Elk had killed the bald man who fled to the trees and then shot Curly Red during their standoff.

Then I owe this man my life. Red Elk smiled knowingly.

"Why did the Spirits tell you to follow me?"

"The Spirits told me you needed help. They told me if I helped you that they would honor my request," Red Elk said.

"Request for what?"

"That is between me and the Spirits. We will catch the wagon tomorrow evening, they won't make good time in the rain."

"Did the also Spirits tell you all that?"

"No. I saw the wagon head south early this morning as you were leaving town, and there are rainclouds in the west. Those will pass over tonight and there are more beyond," Red Elk said. The Crow shifted down into his bedroll and put his back to the fire.

Brett waited a few minutes staring into the thin flames. Then he rolled out his own bedroll and pulled his hat down over his eyes. Soon enough he too was asleep.

8

Brett and Red Elk set out well before dawn. The wagon had just short of a full day's head start on them, but Red Elk said they'd catch up before dark.

The road was muddy and pockmarked with clear shallow puddles. Red Elk's foretelling of last night's weather, one line of storms followed by another, had proven true.

The Crow spoke little as they rode; Brett was content to travel in thought and silence. He'd seen Indians before, Cheyenne mostly, but only in passing. He didn't remember ever speaking to one, much less having one as a traveling companion.

What do you talk about with an Indian?

They made Shell Creek by noon where the trail branched off, one path leading south toward Worland and the other east up and over the pass. As expected, the wagon turned east. Its tracks were plain in the rain-softened ground. They followed.

The trail slowly lifted up above the open plain. It climbed through towering pines and scattered boulders, broken off from the mountains above like so many lost teeth. Though it was still spring, only a trace of snow remained in the pass. The summer was shaping up to be a hot one. There was more snow higher up near the peaks where the drifts had been deeper, but it too was melting fast, trickling from tiny drops into rivulets and then finally merging into the frothing creek itself. Crossing over to the east side of the pass they saw a moose and her newborn calf. Lower down a small herd of shaggy elk were nipping at tender green shoots.

"Life has returned to the mountains," Red Elk said.

"Yes," Brett answered. "We will catch them before evening?"

The Crow nodded. "What will you do when we find them?"

"I don't know," Brett answered truthfully.

Red Elk gave him a long look, "You had better know soon."

They stopped mid-afternoon to rest the horses for a bit and ate dried jerky and some hard biscuits. They refilled their canteens in the stream. Brett didn't know the name of this one. He didn't know much of these southern slopes, but Red Elk called it the Little Buffalo.

Descending as they traveled now, Brett studied the country ahead. There were more trees further down aspen, lodgepole pine, juniper, and cottonwood along the frothy creeks. Beyond them down in the plains was the trail from Cheyenne up to Sheridan. The wagon might turn there or it might strike out directly across the empty plains for the Dakotas.

It was twilight when Red Elk drew up suddenly. They were near the mountain's base and through the screen of trees Brett thought he could make out flickers from a fire.

"We are here," the Crow said.

"We'll slip in close and see how many there are," Brett stepped off his horse and tied it along with the pack animal to a stubby pine. He drew his rifle from its scabbard and then cracked the breech.

One in the chamber. He was ready.

Red Elk has his own rifle, an older Sharps model. He drew a long fat cartridge from a pouch on his belt and placed it in the rifle. He looked at Brett, nodded, and they crept forward.

The trees were thick and dark; Brett did his best to avoid fallen limbs. Red Elk moved like a ghost, completely without sound. They were close when the Crow stopped and eased down to one knee beside a tall pine. Brett did his best to imitate him.

There were three men at the fire, one held a half-empty bottle of whiskey and was belting out a dance-hall tune. He alternated between the words and howls at the moon. A second man wheezed through a harmonica, trying and failing miserably to match the off-key notes of both the howling and singing. The third man was quiet. Hunched over and hat pulled down low, he sat on a fallen log staring toward the group of chained women and one in particular. Brett recognized her immediately. It was the same young girl that gave him the hard glare when he was leaving the warehouse. She stood, chin up and defiant, glaring daggers at the third man.

"Billy, Billy, come on and have a drink," the singing man said between breaths. He offered the bottle to the third man.

Billy took the bottle without taking his eyes off the Indian girl. He drank a long pull and then passed it back without looking.

"Charlie, that harmonica sounds like you're strangling it," the singer said.

"Shut up Jim. Better than your singing," Charlie answered. He took a breath and went back to screeching on the instrument.

These last two, Charlie and Billy, Brett recognized their voices. *The two from the freight house.*

Billy stood up suddenly. "Jim, I'm taking this one off. I don't like the way she looks at me."

Jim laughed. "She looks at everyone like that. Davis said not to spoil them."

"I'm taking her off Jim. Won't be no spoiling I'm just going to teach her a lesson."

"Best watch yourself. She might be teaching you the lesson," Jim said. "She looks meaner than a rattler. Take one of the others."

"I'm taking this one," Billy said. "And she's going to know better than to look at me like I'm some kinda worm."

He moved toward the women. They shrank back from him, all but the defiant girl. She kept her eyes steady on him and only him. He took a key from his breast pocket and unlocked her chain from the others. He snapped it a hard pop and it jerked at the collar around her neck. The girl winced in pain, but managed to hold her stare. The skin under her collar was red and bruised.

"Think you're tough huh? I'll put you in your place little squaw," Billy said. He smirked at her and—chain in hand—hauled her away from the firelight.

Suddenly Brett wasn't sure what to do. Should he warn these men and ask them to release the women? If he did they'd refuse and then they would know he and Red Elk were here. Still it didn't sit right killing a man without warning. Even as he thought of that girl, dragged by the neck out into the brush, his thoughts raced.

How am I going to make one of these men testify against Judd?

He touched Red Elk on the shoulder and nodded toward the two men. He tapped himself and then pointed to the singer. Red Elk nodded and aimed his rifle at the man with the harmonica.

A scream came from the darkness. A woman's voice, sharp and in great pain.

"Give 'er hell Billy," Charlie said, and both men at the fire laughed.

Right then Brett made up his mind. All thoughts of Davis Judd evaporated. He took aim on Charlie, putting his sights dead center on the man's chest. He squeezed the trigger and the night erupted in gunfire when Red Elk took his own shot.

Charlie took the bullet in his chest and inch from his middle shirt button. He jerked back. The whiskey fell out of his hand and splashed into the fire and the light flared up bright and hot.

The second man took the Sharp's huge bullet and flew back like he'd been hit by a charging bull.

Brett levered the rifle for a fresh round and was on his feet sprinting toward the direction of the scream.

Another long scream tore through the night; this one sounded more of rage than hurt.

Following the sound, Brett crashed through a clump of brush.

Rough branches tore at his face and clothes and then he seemed to fall into a sort of clearing. He saw the girl first.

She was stripped to the waist, sitting square on top of Billy's chest, holding a wet-looking rock the size of a loaf of bread high above her head. Hair whipping loose and wild, she screamed and brought the rock crashing down. She lifted it and brought it down again and then again and again. Each time there was a wet, smacking sound.

Keeping well back, Brett circled around to one side until he could see Billy. The man's skull was caved in, his face a mask of blood and mush. He was obviously dead.

Finally, long after he'd lost count of how many times she'd struck the dead man, the girl sagged forward. Her hate-filled screams dropped into low wails and she began to sob.

Unsure of what to do, Brett waited. He stayed well clear of her.

She'll lash out at anything that gets close.

He looked at Billy's ruined skull. The girl released the rock and it rolled from her fingers coated in sticky blood. He did not want to be on the receiving end of that.

After a long time there was a rattling noise in the brush. *No doubt Red Elk and the other freed women are looking for us.* The girl stopped crying at the sound; she rubbed at her eyes to hide her tears, but that only left bloodstains. She drew her blouse up over her shoulders. Only then did she see him.

Face expressionless, she looked in his eyes for a long moment. He saw the hatred there, but beneath that the deep sense of pain.

Brett lifted his hand, palm open. "It's alright, that's just Red Elk. He has your friends free by now," he explained. He spoke a little louder than necessary, hoping the Crow would hear him.

If she understood she gave no sign. Her eyes left his only for the briefest moment when she picked up the bloody rock and held it against the dead man's chest. Then she looked him full in the face and her chin lifted ever so slightly.

Red Elk came into the clearing then along with one of the older women. He eyed the woman carefully and Brett saw a hint of something there. *Relief?* It was gone then like a whisper among a strong wind.

"You are unhurt?" he asked.

"Yes. But I'm not sure about her," Brett gestured. "The other two are dead?"

"Very."

Brett swore. *So much for using these men against Davis Judd. No one would ever believe just my word and that of these women.* He'd have to find another way to run the rancher off.

Red Elk looked at the girl for a time and the older woman moved to comfort her. Red Elk bent down, took Billy's key from his pocket, and removed the shackle from around the girl's neck. The chain dropped clear with a loud rattle. Red Elk stood and paused for a moment then said, "Let us go back to the fire."

Brett stood slowly. Though the older woman tried to comfort her, the girl's eyes continued to hold his. Her fingers squeezed the rock until her knuckles turned white.

Red Elk led the way back to the fire where the other women sat huddled around for warmth. They started to rise when the two approached but the Crow calmed them in their own language. Each eyed Brett distrustfully when they were close. The two dead men lay as they'd fallen.

Brett took Charlie by the arms and hauled him back into the brush some distance away. Red Elk moved the other.

"We will load up and travel. This place is not safe. Bears will smell their blood," Red Elk said. "I know a place nearby."

It sounded good to Brett. He had no desire to be anywhere near the dead men.

Brett hitched up the horses as Red Elk had never done it before. They returned to the fire and started loading up the supplies. Finally, Red Elk coaxed the women into the wagon helping each climb up in turn. They were finishing with the wagon when the last two women emerged from the woods.

The girl took a seat near the others but continued to glare at him.

"Do you want to drive the wagon?" Brett asked.

"I will," Red Elk said. He paused to look at the girl then at Brett. "I believe that one might try to kill you."

Instead of going back toward the pass they continued east. The wagon wheels creaked and popped as they dropped down out of the trees. The moon was out and just bright enough to see the trail by.

They traveled for an hour, the going was slow, and then Red Elk turned off the trail and brought them to a clump of trees down in a little notch out of the cold mountain wind. Brett unhooked the team. There was a creek nearby and he watered each of the horses.

When he returned Red Elk had a fire going and the women were cooking a haunch of deer over it.

"Coffee?" Brett asked.

"No," the Crow said. "I do not know how."

"You've never made coffee?"

"I have not."

"Have you ever tasted coffee?"

"I have not."

Brett walked toward the supplies piled near the wagon. The guards would have had the makings.

Cowboys always had coffee.

As he moved the women shuffled away from him like he was a porcupine or rattlesnake. He found the grounds, then the pot, and soon had coffee brewing over the fire.

He sat on a log beside Red Elk. The Crow was cleaning the Sharps. The cartridges for those older guns were notoriously dirty.

"Are they of your tribe?" Brett asked.

"Cheyenne," Red Elk said. He nodded to the girl, the fierce one. "All but that one. She is half-Crow."

"Half-Crow?"

"Her mother was Crow, her father Cheyenne."

"Is that common among the tribes?"

"No."

"Does she have a name?" Brett asked.

"In the white tongue it is Morning Song."

"Morning Song, that sounds nice actually."

Red Elk gave him a look. "Not Morning like dawn or rising sun, Mourning as in a song for the dead."

"Ohh, that doesn't sound so good."

"No." Red Elk finished with the rifle.

Brett moved to the coffee pot and the girl's eyes lifted to meet his. There was so much anger in them his heart skipped. He crouched and poured himself a cup. Then he eased back up to the log and sat down.

"She will kill you if she gets the chance," Red Elk said. He looked at Mourning Song.

"You said that before. Why would she?"

"She hates you and all whites. There is a great burning anger in her. An evil Spirit," Red Elk turned to give him a solemn look. "Do not turn your back on her."

"We saved her though. Her and the others." Brett didn't understand it. All whites certainly weren't the same. Just as he was coming to realize that not all Indians were the same.

"It does not matter. You are a white and you are an enemy."

"What do we do with them?"

"What do you mean?"

"We can't leave them here. Someone else might come along and take them just like those men," Brett said. He didn't want to be stuck with a half-dozen women, one of whom wanted to crater his skull in with a rock, but he didn't want to abandon them either. "How far is it to their reservation?"

"Two days ride. South and west," he looked over at the sitting wagon. "Three days with that."

Three days. Another two or three even to get back to Pryor. Brett didn't want to be gone from the ranch for so long. Still there was no other choice, and he hadn't made up his mind what to do about getting his father's ranch back. He'd failed completely here, and he needed to find a way to hurt Davis Judd. Something he could take and then exchange in order to buy his ranch back. He wouldn't trade a wagonload of women for it of that he was certain.

I need leverage over the man.

"We'll return them to the reservation then," Brett said.

"If that is what you want," Red Elk said.

Brett looked at the girl; she was glaring at him again. He shuddered. He imagined Mourning Song sitting on his chest, hair whipping wild, screaming, eyes surging with rage and hate, holding that blood-drenched rock high above her head, and then it coming crashing down.

Not a good way to go. What kind of woman is she?

————

THE JOURNEY TOOK every bit of three days to reach the reservation and, whatever his expectations, Brett was sorely disappointed in the place. It looked like an empty desolate land with scattered clumps of sage and the occasional stunted pine dotting the landscape. There were a few squat mountains scattered about—only hills really—nothing like the majestic Bighorns or the steel gray sawtooth peaks of the Wind River Range further south.

They were crossing a flat expanse when the first brave rode into view atop the nearest hill, stopped, and looked down at them. Brett studied him in turn.

The brave wore a deep blue shirt and buckskin leggings. He held a long rifle, butt planted firmly on one leg.

Brett wanted no trouble with these people, only to return their women and then go on home. Without pausing or bothering to look, Red Elk kept his gaze on the road ahead. Brett tried to mimic his disregard. He'd heard Indians respected bravery.

In moments though a second and third brave took up positions beside the first, and then suddenly there were four and five and six. Still more came on. The warriors neither moved nor spoke, only watched from the skyline, sitting their horses still as statues.

Beneath the brim of his hat, Brett watched them back. Casually, he reached down and eased the thong off his Colt. He counted two dozen braves total.

More than enough to kill us.

He brought his horse up closer to the wagon. "What now?"

Red Elk turned and looked at the braves as if seeing them for the first time. After a quick glance, he turned back to the road ahead and returned to ignoring them. "We keep on. Their village is ahead down near the river. Show them no fear."

"We'll drop the women off there?"

Red Elk was non-committal, "We will see."

Brett tried to follow Red Elk's lead, but now and then his eyes swung off to the hill and those stoic faced warriors.

Are they deciding how best to come at us?

Burdened as they were with a wagon and a load of women, it wouldn't be much of a fight. More a quick slaughter.

Mercifully, the wagon creaked around the hill's base. Brett glanced behind quickly to see if the warriors followed. Single-file the braves descended to the valley floor and then fanned out in a long line behind the wagon.

Red Elk kept his eyes locked forward. "Best not to look at them," he advised.

Brett took the advice. He noticed then that each of the women was doing likewise. *Come to think of it they never even looked in their direction.* He expected that some of the women riding in the wagon would have brothers or husbands among the braves, but not one had called out.

What a strange people.

From the corner of his eye he saw one woman who wasn't looking forward. The girl, Mourning Song, looked squarely at him. Today her eyes didn't seem quite so hard. She wasn't glaring, merely watching, studying him as if he were some new sort of animal she'd just discovered. Though the change wasn't great, it seemed almost pleasant by comparison.

Finally, the Cheyenne village came into view. It too wasn't much. In a line along both banks of the river stood around twenty sun-whitened teepees. A hint of gray smoke rose from each. There were only a few people in sight, mostly older, hunched down in their robes near a teepee or sitting beside a campfire. Dogs and children roamed the village, and there were strips of meat drying on a number of tall wooden racks.

The wagon was less than a half-mile out when the braves let out a long whoop. Brett fought down the urge to draw his gun and slap spurs to his horse. He flattened his hand against his leg.

Show them no fear. If they wanted to kill us they would have done it already.

The braves continued to whoop and then came the thunder of hooves as they swept on past.

The village came alive with the chorus as men and women emptied from the teepees and gathered outside. An ancient man with a long white headdress moved out front and center.

The braves split into two groups, one veering around on each side of the crowd, circling back until they faced the wagon and then stopping. They sat their horses and continued whooping, stopping only when the old Chief raised a hand.

Red Elk pulled the wagon to a stop almost fifty paces short of the Chief. He eased down, circled to the back, and offered his hand to one of the women. She took it and descended the wagon like a queen, then waited beside Red Elk. The next woman did the same, as did all the others. If they were excited they hid it well.

Brett couldn't see even a hint of it.

For his own part, Brett slid down off his horse. If he decided to run for it now, they'd have him before his tired horse made a hundred strides. He stood off a bit to one side away from the others and keeping his left hand free.

I will not go down without a fight.

To his surprise the last woman off the wagon, Mourning Song, took Red Elk's hand, climbed down, and then came around and—instead of joining the others—came and stood beside him, close enough to touch if he chose. She stared straight at the Chief.

Brett wasn't sure what had just happened, but several of the braves were eyeing him hard now. *Likely this girl's brothers*, he reasoned, *or husband*. She didn't seem like the married type, but he knew little of such things.

He swallowed and felt a bead of sweat gather on his forehead.

Red Elk spoke to the Chief then. Brett didn't understand a word of it. As he spoke though the Crow gestured first to himself, then to the women, and finally to Brett.

Suddenly Brett became acutely aware that he didn't really know Red Elk that well. They'd only met a few days ago. Still, if Red Elk had wanted him dead there were plenty of other opportunities. The Crow could have let Curly Red kill him or he could have just shot him from cover like he dropped the third man down by the river.

Brett eyed the big Sharps sitting propped up in the wagon.

A bullet from that would make a bad hole in a man. Especially up close. He'd seen what it did to the harmonica player.

The Chief stopped talking and Brett noticed all the Cheyenne were now looking at him. Red Elk gestured for him to approach. Staying a step behind, Mourning Song walked with him.

"This is Chief Watches Deer. He is grateful for the return of his women," Red Elk said.

Several of the braves bared their teeth at Brett.

"The braves say that the white men took the women as they were out collecting acorns."

"They don't seem so grateful," Brett said.

"They would very much like to kill you," Watches Deer smiled and said in perfect English.

Stunned, Brett could only look at him.

"Red Elk is a powerful medicine man though," the Chief suddenly said. "And he says it was your idea to free these women and then to return them to us. So you are a guest in my village. Be welcomed." He went on to say something in Cheyenne and the braves backed off. One of them spit at the ground near Brett's feet. With that the tension broke and the crowd started yelling for joy as the freed women rejoined their smiling families.

There was one woman though that no one greeted. Mourning Song stepped past Brett to approach the Chief alone.

The Chief gave her a sorrowful look; a tear ran down his cheek. In a low voice he spoke to her, and she bowed her head to stare at the ground. Then Watches Deer reached out and touched her cheek.

Brett had never seen her act like that. *Three days we've traveled and I've never seen her act anything other than defiant or proud. And angry, don't forget angry.*

The Chief said something more in Cheyenne and Mourning Song started away toward a smiling woman with white-streaked hair. Briefly they hugged and then wandered off.

Her mother or grandmother no doubt.

Watches Deer turned to Red Elk and spoke in English for Brett's benefit. "I would be honored, old enemy, if you would join me in my lodge for a meal."

"It is we who would be honored, great Chief," Red Elk accepted. "In the morning we must leave."

The Chief nodded. "It is good to stay tonight. The wind whispers of rain again. I will have a place prepared for you. Leave your horses with Laughing Dog." He gestured toward a young brave nearby.

Brett handed the reins over. He was eager to leave, but he'd often heard Indians were proud and he did not wish to offend them.

"Yes," Red Elk said. He looked at the sky. "It does look like rain."

"When you get so old as me, you don't need to look. You can feel it in your bones," the Chief grinned.

Watches Deer started into the village and Red Elk fell in beside him. In their wake Brett followed.

Passing between teepees with still-weeping families, Red Elk and Watches Deer spoke in Cheyenne. They crossed the village slowly; the old Chief carried quite a limp.

"Would you know how I got this limp?" he suddenly said.

"Yes," Brett said.

"When I was a younger man and my people still roamed the land of my ancestors my father was a powerful medicine man. He and the Chief and I met with the one you call Two Moons at the Little Bighorn. I fought the yellow-hair and his soldiers there. We fought well and won the day, but one of the yellow-hair's soldiers shot me in the knee."

"Custer's men?" Brett asked. Every westerner knew the story of the Seventh Cavalry.

"Yes," Watches Deer said. "Crazy Horse himself said it was a great honor to be wounded in battle with the yellow-hair. After we sighed the treaty with the Great White Father, one of the army doctors offered to remove the bullet, but I worried it would offend the Spirits. After all it did me no lasting harm."

"And now?" Red Elk asked.

"And now I regret that I didn't let him. It hurts like hell," Watches Deer laughed and Brett couldn't help but join him. He found himself liking the old Cheyenne.

Finally they arrived at the Chief's lodge.

Red Elk lifted the flap and Watches Deer stepped inside. He motioned for Brett to follow. There was a tiny fire in the center of the room and Brett took a seat across from Watches Deer. Red Elk sat down beside him.

A woman entered and Brett looked up at her. For a second, he froze. Morning Song had her hair braided back now and she'd found time to change her clothes. Without the scowl she looked almost serene. She did not look at him. Instead she held her gaze down at the floor. She knelt down beside the Chief and held out a thick piece of leathery buffalo hide with smoked meat and coarse yellow bread laying on it.

Following Red Elk's lead, Brett tore off a piece of bread and then a chunk of meat. Morning Song still didn't acknowledge them. She set the food aside, then stood and crossed the little room, only to return with a waterskin and three tin cups.

"At my age I find a cup is easier to drink from," the Chief said. He looked at Mourning Song. "Leave us. I will speak to these men."

She set the waterskin down beside the food and left without speaking. On the way out, where the Chief couldn't see her, she glanced once at Brett. It was quick, but the look was there and full of...what exactly? Not the dark brooding anger he normally received nor the strange studying look she'd given him earlier. Something else entirely.

What did Red Elk say to these people about me?

"There is change in the wind. Always change," the Chief was saying.

"Change is not always for the best," Red Elk said.

Watches Deer nodded. "It comes regardless. How are your people?"

"They continue," Red Elk shrugged. "The old ways are gone. The great herds are gone with them. The young men do not listen to their elders. They rattle their arrows and shake their spears. They long to return to the days of old."

"Those days will not return, I think."

"The young do not listen."

"My son felt the same," Watches Deer said. "He was a proud warrior, straight and true. He grew up on stories of the clever coyote and the wise shaggy buffalo. He wanted to ride the plains and hunt and visit the high places. He was born too late. He was born to a dying people."

"We are all dying," Red Elk said.

"My son is gone now. A dark Spirit has taken my family. First my son, his wife," Watches Deer paused to give Red Elk a sorrowful look, "and then my granddaughter's husband. All lost. All taken in the winter by the coughing. Only my wife and I remain and now the evil Spirit dwells within my granddaughter."

The Chief looked to the teepee flap where Mourning Song had departed.

Granddaughter...Mourning Song...She is the Chief's granddaughter then.

"You have tried a cleansing?" Red Elk asked. His voice carried strong emotion. *Did he lose a loved one in the same way?*

"Of course," Watches Deer said. "But the old ways do not work anymore. The Spirits have abandoned us as we have abandoned the land. My people fear Mourning Song. They say she has defied the Spirits and brought this evil down upon us. They will not be glad of her return."

Red Elk nodded once then turned to the fire. The light reflected in his obsidian eyes, and his expression was solemn.

Brett gazed into the flames as well. His thoughts drifted to Mourning Song. *A dark Spirit.* That explained why there was only the old woman to meet her when they arrived. That must have been the Chief's wife. *To lose your mother and father and then husband all in one winter.* Despite his own hardships, Brett couldn't imagine it.

In a way, he'd lost as much, but hers had all been in the span of only a few months. *And now her people think she caused it somehow.*

Red Elk finally stood and Brett followed suit. The Crow took the Chief's hand and thanked him for his hospitality. Then they were outside where Mourning Song waited to guide them to their own lodge. Red Elk seemed to ignore her completely, but Brett couldn't keep from seeing her differently now.

While they walked he noticed the way the others in the village drew back a step. Women clutched their children a little tighter at their approach. The warriors gave them hard looks. He'd seen this earlier when they first arrived and assumed either he or Red Elk had been the cause, but it was her they were frightened of. One of their own.

Mourning Song stopped at a teepee, turned, and left without a word. Red Elk lifted the flap and Brett followed him inside. He was relieved to see his saddle and packs there along with the rifle he'd stolen from Judd's freight office.

Red Elk unrolled his blankets and immediately lay down to sleep. The Crow seemed even more thoughtful than usual this evening.

Brett tried sleeping, but his own thoughts kept returning to Mourning Song. They'd saved her from Judd's men and returned her to the tribe, but was she that much better off? Her people didn't want her. They believed she'd somehow killed first her parents and then husband.

Her chains may be gone, but in a way she's still a prisoner.

The Cheyenne were superstitious, Brett didn't believe for a moment that an evil Spirit was the true cause; to him it sounded like whooping cough. He never could have explained that to them though.

He lay awake wondering what would become of the fierce young woman. Watches Deer was old but no doubt the Chief was protecting her as best he could. That couldn't continue forever though. A new Chief might cast her out or marry her off into another tribe just to be rid of her.

Brett remembered the way she'd looked at him from that cold iron cage back in Pryor. Whatever happened she was a fighter.

9

It was still dark when Brett and Red Elk started out the next day. They rode north and a little east aiming for the western slope of the Bighorns. Once they were well away from the village, they abandoned the wagon down in a dry creekbed where it wouldn't be found. They set loose the team where they could find their way to join one of the area's mustang herds.

In addition to slowing them down, the wagon would only have tied them to the trails and drawn questions.

They kept to the low places, avoiding attention, skirting the grassy hills and ridges despite the added distance. Around noon, Red Elk reigned up. They were near the base of the Bighorns on a broad plain, a sweeping expanse of gray-green sage behind and the welcoming shelter of cool pines and shady juniper just ahead. Brett looked back over their trail toward a little trace of dust.

"She follows," Red Elk said.

"Who?" Brett asked.

The Crow said nothing. He dismounted and walked his horse beneath the edge of the trees. Then he found a soft spot among the mat of discarded pine needles and sat to rest in the shade.

Brett watched the dust slowly grow nearer and nearer until he saw a single figure riding a palomino pony. Mourning Song. Her gaze held steady on the spot where he and Red Elk had entered the trees and she rode with purpose, neither quick nor slow.

Brett couldn't imagine why she'd followed after them.

She ignored him when he stepped from the trees and offered her his canteen. She rode by without so much as a look his way and spoke in quick Cheyenne to Red Elk. He answered and gestured with his hands, but she only shook her head. He spoke again and she answered with a single word, setting her jaw in a hard line. Red Elk stared at her. His look was hard enough to crack stone, but glare-for-glare she matched him.

Finally, the Crow let out an exasperated sigh. He spoke a few quick words in Cheyenne and Mourning Song's chin lifted as if she'd won something.

"Why is she here?" Brett asked.

"She says—" Red Elk paused to reconsider her. "She says she owes you a life. She intends to repay it so she can be free."

"That isn't necessary. I'd rather she just went back to her people."

"I told her that," Red Elk said. He slanted his eyes at her. "She took it as an insult to her honor. She is stubborn as any brave and twice the fool."

The Crow swung up into his saddle and started out.

Brett climbed onto his horse and hurried to catch up. Mourning Song followed, but remained a dozen horse-lengths back.

"Wait, what do we do with her?"

"We?" Red Elk said. "This is your problem."

"My problem?"

"Yes. Are you going back to your cabin in the mountain?"

"I am," Brett said. He wasn't sure of his next move, but he wanted to check on his place and make sure Judd's men hadn't found it. So far he'd been lucky; that kind of luck couldn't hold forever.

"I will leave you now then. There is something I must do for my people and then I will return."

"How will you find me?"

Red Elk turned to regard him for a long moment. Brett felt foolish.

The old man has his ways.

"What about her?"

Red Elk squinted at the girl. "I believe she will go with you. Do not sleep too deeply, she might still try to kill you."

With that Red Elk cut to the right and started up and over the mountains.

Brett sat for a time and looked back at Mourning Song. She stared at him, face impassive and hard as stone.

What am I going to do with her? He couldn't be responsible for a woman. He had a ranch to win back.

With nothing else to do, he started on toward the ranch and the mining shack.

After traveling the whole day in complete silence, they made camp a few miles south of Pryor. Brett unsaddled his horse and pick-eted it and his packhorse in a little meadow. He thought to care for the palomino, but Mourning Song had already done it herself. Then he settled down to a cold dinner, some hardtack from his saddlebags, while she ate some food of her own.

After a restless night's sleep, Brett woke early. Mourning Song lay sleeping in her blankets and he rattled his spurs to wake her.

The mining shack was just as he'd left it. He circled it once, looking for any strange tracks and found none.

He let both his horses and Mourning Song's palomino loose in the corral. He fed a few handfuls of corn to each and all three ate like they'd never seen the stuff before.

With her bedding and other gear in her arms, Mourning Song watched him all the while. He headed to the shack and she paused outside the door, staring at the building as if it were a buzzing snake. Brett dropped his saddle on the floor, made a second trip for the spare horse's pack and saddlebags, and then checked the shack over.

His money remained hidden in a loose panel on one wall and his other supplies were all as he'd left them. With the reward from Curly

Red, added to what remained from Davis Judd's house, he had a good sum.

He went back out to Mourning Song.

"It's just a building, a lodge like one of your teepees. Nothing to be afraid of."

She looked dubiously from him to the building and then back again.

Maybe she's never seen a building before. Then he remembered the terrible anger in her eyes from inside the cage in Judd's freight office.

"It's alright, it won't hurt you." He tried to keep his voice calm and even. Mourning Song refused to move though.

Finally, he gave up and went on inside. In a few moments he had a fire going in the little stove and started putting food on to cook. He glanced over his shoulder at times, but Mourning Song stood just as she had and only peered in back at him.

He dished up a plateful of beans, a slab of seared beef to go with them, then poured a cup of coffee, and carried it all out to the porch for her. He doubted she'd ever had coffee either. For a time she only looked at the steaming food.

She'll think I'm trying to poison her. She had to be hungry though, they hadn't eaten since the morning and then only a cold meal of coarse bread and dried meat.

He heaped up a plate for himself. Then he carried it out to the porch. He sat on a round of wood, took out his fork and knife, and started to eat.

Mourning Song watched him for a long time; she drew a knife out of her belt and started over.

"No need to stab a fellow," he said.

She smiled, the first time he'd ever seen one, and she snatched up her plate and then retreated back away from him. She kept smiling as she ate and, other than the knife held menacingly in her hands, it was a pleasant look.

After finishing her food, she took a swig of the coffee and immediately spat it out. She peered into the mug, gave him a narrow-eyed look, watched him drink from his own, and then tried again.

Disgustedly, she spit it out a second time and he laughed.

She jumped up and waved the knife at him. Her eyes were wild now. He stopped laughing and took another sip.

Mourning Song came forward a step. The knife blade caught the sun's dying light and flashed orange.

"Easy now. Calm down," Brett raised his open palms. "It's just coffee. See, I'm drinking it." Keeping his eyes on her, he picked up his mug and took another mouthful.

She stammered something in Cheyenne.

"Fine have it your way," he rose slowly and started toward the door. She shot back a step, knife still held ready.

She spoke again in quick Cheyenne and then spit on the ground.

Brett went into the shack then. She moved to the threshold, glaring in, keeping the knife held out dangerously between them. She looked around inside, taking it all in quickly, then spit on the floor.

Slowly, she withdrew from the house. "Weak," she said.

"What did you say?" Brett said. "Do you speak English? Can you understand me?"

She retreated further.

Her grandfather speaks English. It shouldn't surprise me if she does as well.

Mourning Song refused to say more. Without taking her eyes off him or lowering the knife, she withdrew to her bedroll, hoisted it up over her shoulder, and walked away toward a copse of evergreens.

Brett watched her go. He gathered up the plates and cups and started inside. Then just to show her, he took a long swig of her coffee. He closed the door and unrolled his bedding so his feet were brushing up against it. He kept his Colt close by his side.

"Do not sleep deeply," Red Elk had said. "She might try to kill you."

"Well I don't plan on it," he muttered and closed his eyes. He also didn't plan on shooting a woman, but that one was half wildcat. She might not give him a choice.

———

BRETT ROSE EARLY the following morning. He made a quick breakfast, saddled his horse, and started toward out toward Youngston. It had been some time since he'd seen the Sweeneys. He didn't see Mourning Song and wondered if she'd gone back to her people.

Probably decided I tried to poison her with coffee. He wasn't sure if it was wise for her to travel alone, but he couldn't do anything for it.

When he arrived Gideon Sweeney was out front, shirt darkened by sweat and with the sleeves rolled up to his pale elbows, digging on a posthole. His sons were further down, each sweating over holes of their own.

"New fence?" Brett asked.

"New fence," Gideon nodded. His expression was serious. "Last week James Tolliver was down in Pryor. He couldn't wait for the trip to Billings. They waited until he'd bought his supplies and started toward home and then Kip Lane and some of the men he rides with caught him just outside town. They beat him. Doctor Wahlquist said he's lucky to be alive, but he's lost all sight in his left eye. Wahlquist doesn't think his vision will ever return."

"Kip Lane and his crew?" Brett asked.

Gideon nodded. "His wife and son were with him, they saw the whole thing."

Brett knew the Tollivers. More than once they had come by to do business with Gideon when he was on the mend and several times later when he'd stopped by for a visit. They were nice people—James wasn't too much older than himself. Their son was a little dark-haired boy with freckles and shining happy eyes like Sarah, his mother. She'd been pregnant last time he'd seen them. He wondered if she'd had the baby. A baby who'd almost lost his father because of Kip Lane and his thugs.

"What will you do?" Brett asked.

Gideon gazed out into the east. The wind whistled through the trees nearby. "I don't know. The Governor hasn't answered my letters.

I'm afraid this beautiful Wyoming is not ready for folk like us. Perhaps one day it will be."

For a time neither spoke. Brett's horse stamped impatiently.

"Will you get down and join us for lunch? I'm sure Lisa would enjoy seeing you."

"Not today," Brett said. He very much wanted to see Lisa; she'd been much on his mind the last few days. Suddenly though he was sick. He couldn't stop thinking about James Tolliver and his wife and children. Blind in one eye, according to the Doctor. He couldn't imagine what had been taken away from them.

He wanted to do something. But what? For the first time in months he didn't want to get his ranch back. Or at least he didn't only want to get his ranch back. He wanted to even up the score for the Tollivers too.

Davis Judd brought these thugs into the country. Now they needed to be cleaned out.

"I'm heading to Pryor," Brett said.

"That is not wise," Gideon said. "Brett, they will kill you. There are too many of them."

"Maybe. But someone has to do something."

"Listen, just wait and listen and think for a moment please," Gideon said. "When Jane and I first settled into the Promised Land I was a much younger man. We fought the desert. We fought the locusts and the wolves and the bears and even the weather itself. The second winter almost wiped us out. It was so cold we lost half our livestock. Hens sitting, frozen dead on their nests. Some of the horses lost their ears."

Gideon held up his right hand, fingers spread. His ring finger was half the length it should have been.

"That's how I almost lost this finger. I had to go out and try to keep the calves alive. The ground was so cold they froze to it if they didn't stand up occasionally. One day while I was out with them it started to snow and I became lost. I floundered around in a circle and then, as luck would have it, I stumbled against the barn. I threw my hand out to stop my fall and my finger got caught between a couple of the boards. To get free I had to cut the end off at the knuckle."

Gideon's eyes glazed over as he paused. He continued.

"Losing the finger saved my life. I was incoherent when it happened. Snowblind. Stumbling against that barn, cutting off my finger, it woke me up enough to find the house."

Brett studied him.

"My point is sometimes bad things happen in order to save us from something worse. This all has to be for some greater purpose. It may be that losing your ranch is the best thing that could have happened to you. After all you've been through you are so fortunate to be alive. Take your life and go live it. Your parents wouldn't want you throwing it away seeking vengeance. They would want you to live."

Brett thought for a moment. He started his horse toward Pryor. He lifted a hand to the brim of his hat. "I'll see you around Gideon."

With that he spurred his horse away.

Gideon Sweeney was not a coward. Far from it. Brett doubted the man was afraid of anything. But he didn't understand. This was all just beyond him. The threat of Davis Judd and his gunmen wasn't like the weather or the locusts or the desert. They would never stop coming.

They had to be stopped and before it was done more men would die.

Once he was away from Youngston, Brett slowed his mare to a walk. Then he left the trail and rested in a stand of aspen for a time so that it was dark when he came into Pryor. The darkness would better serve his purposes.

The streets were empty as he passed by the first saloon. Tonight it was quiet, not the kind of place Kip Lane and his friends would be.

Across the street, the second saloon was loud and boisterous with laughter and singing and cursing coming from within. Brett dismounted behind Judd's new bank and tied his horse in a loose knot where he could escape quickly. He drew his rifle from its scabbard and checked to make sure it was full. He slipped the thong off his Colt and then jammed the second pistol he'd taken off Curly Red's friend into his belt behind his back.

His plan, if it could be called such, was simple. He'd walk into the saloon, spot Kip and his friends, and then open up with the rifle. When it was empty he'd switch to his pistols and fight his way back out to his waiting horse.

A dark and narrow alleyway separated the bank and saloon. Brett paused at the edge of it and took a breath. He steeled himself against what he had to do.

Just get in, shoot as fast as you can, and get out. He could retreat first to the corner of the bank, and then if Lane or one of his men showed himself he'd throw a few more rounds back at them before racing away.

He spared a moment to think of the Tolliver family and what they had gone through. Kip Lane was a dog that had to be put down.

He's really just the tool though, and once he's gone Judd will just bring in more, I've got to find a way to get him as well.

Brett took a step toward the saloon and heard a noise from down the alley. He froze. If anyone saw him now he might lose his only advantage. He heard a retching noise, saw an outline of someone—a woman—bent over double on her hands and knees, long hair falling down over her face. She started to cry.

"Damn him," she said. "Damn all men."

She shifted up into a kneeling position and wiped her mouth with the back of her hand.

Brett smelled the alcohol and vomit. He recognized the voice though, knew it well.

"Allie?" he whispered.

She didn't respond. To steady herself, she stuck a hand out to the saloon wall and slowly climbed to her feet. A bottle shone in the alley and she reached down and picked it up by the long neck. The contents sloshed noisily. She tipped it back and took a pull.

She took a weaving step and reached out for the wall's support. She started to fall back again.

Before he could stop himself Brett was at her side. He looped an arm around her waist and half-carried her toward the back of the saloon. There was a little discarded stool and he eased Allie down on it.

The light was better back there and he saw a big yellowing bruise on her cheek and a number of dark purple marks around the delicate skin of her neck.

"Like what you shheee?" she slurred. Her eyes were cloudy and unfocused. "Take me out of this godforsaken place. I'll show you plenty more."

At the smell of her breath, Brett's stomach turned.

"Kip Lane promised me he'd take me away but he lied," she slurred. "Before that I had a nice boy all willing and ready to do whatever I wanted, but Kip...he promised me. He's a real man and he said he'd make me a rich woman and we'd travel to San Francisco or New York or Europe."

A nice boy willing and ready to do whatever I wanted. The words stung. After her betrayal he wouldn't have imagined Allie could still hurt him.

He started to leave. She caught him by the sleeve.

"C'mon love, take me with you."

"I don't know you," Brett said.

"But you like what you shheee," she grinned. "An I know something. I know where there's a lot of money. Lane. He's afraid to take it, but you look big and tough. I bet you're a real man. I bet you could take it for me."

Brett jerked his sleeve free. He had to get to the front of the saloon and kill Lane before she gave him away.

"Awww don't be like that. Forty thousand in gold," she said. "It belongs to Davis Judd and Kip is afraid to cross him. Says he needs Davis and he has bigger plans. Bigger than Forty thousand dollars?"

Allie took another drink and almost fell over.

"Where?" Brett's breath caught. This might be his answer. *If I can get my hands on that much of his money...*

"There's a wagon coming over from Deadwood soon with forty

thousand in gold for Davis Judd. It's from his partner out there. But Lane...Bah...He's afraid to take it."

Forty thousand in gold. With that I could move on and buy a different ranch or I could hire gunmen of my own and run Davis and his crew clear out of Wyoming.

There would be no need for him to fight Judd and his men. There were gunmen in Billings, more in Cheyenne; he could just pay a few of them to take his father's ranch back.

"When exactly is the gold coming?"

"Two weeks from today. By the old trail. Only two guards to keep attention off it," she said. "Take the gold an then take me with you."

"Do you even know who I am?" he said.

She leaned back a bit and looked at him for a long time. Her eyes searched his. The alley was dark, and he knew he'd changed. Long-unshaven, his face was scruffy and harder than it used to be. He'd filled out as well, far heavier in the arms and chest and shoulders from cutting wood. It had been almost half a year since she'd seen him the last time and then he'd been shot and falling to his 'death'.

"You're familiar, but..."

"Why are you with Lane? Why not leave?"

She laughed, a hard bitter sound. "An go where? It takes money to travel. My parents won't take me back after living with him. I had a good boy once. He was weak though. Afraid to fight for what was his."

Weak. That was what she'd thought of him. Brett felt his anger flare up like a bonfire.

"What happened to him?" Brett choked out.

"He died. He couldn't make up his mind on what he wanted an he died." She took another long pull from the bottle. She slipped a little to her left and fell to the ground. She giggled and drew the bottle close against her chest. "Such a good, weak little boy," she crooned.

Fuming, Brett started back toward the front of the saloon. *Weak.* The same word Mourning Song had used. He'd show her weak. He'd drill Kip Lane dead center to send that smiling devil right to hell along with the rest of his gang. That loudmouth bastard back in

Sheridan had learned how weak he was. So did Curly Red's little band and the men guarding the Cheyenne women. He'd prove them wrong. All he had to do was end this.

I will show them weak.

He was halfway up the darkened alley when his plans shattered.

"Help! Help! He attacked me," Allie screamed from behind the saloon.

For a second he hoped no one had heard, but inside everything had gone suddenly silent.

"HELP," Allie screamed again.

Brett raced forward toward the gap. He cleared the alleyway, rounded the bank without slowing, and tore at his horse's reins. At the saloon's front, boots pounded over the boardwalk. He leaped into the saddle, wheeled his horse, and rode hard for the edge of town.

A shot rang out behind him. Turning in the saddle, Brett raised his rifle. He held his fire. He didn't want to shoot at someone he couldn't see. For all he knew it was one of the townsfolk responding to a screaming woman. Men gathered in a knot out front of the saloon. He saw the flash from a rifle and heard the bullet whiz by.

He put three bullets into the saloon, all hit well high of the crowd but men still scrambled for cover. *That'll make them back off a bit.* He straightened back around and slammed the rifle deep into its scabbard.

A pair of men armed with rifles came running out of Judd's freight office just ahead. Brett palmed his Colt and put several rounds into the building. Wood cracked as his bullets struck and the men dove back around the corner.

Then Pryor fell away behind him. His horse was running flat out, hoofbeats drumming a quick rhythm on the hardpacked trail, and Brett didn't slow until they were well out of town. His mind raced. *What to do next?* They would be out searching after him now, Judd's men and likely a few others from town among them. Whatever he did, he couldn't lead them back toward the shack. It was his only refuge.

He cut left off the trail and skirted around the tree-lined edge of a grassy meadow. He found an old game trail and followed it up into the foothills. The trail branched and he took the northernmost path. It rose and then crossed a wide pile of loose shale. His horse scrambled as rocks rattled and slid while he cleared it.

The trail followed a draw then turned back south, doubling over itself but now almost five hundred feet higher up the mountain.

Exhausted and unwilling to ride further in the dark, he camped beneath a huge gnarled pine. He sat alone in the dark thinking about what to do next. Had Allie lied? Had she recognized him the whole time? Or had she just struck out at him after he refused to take her with him?

I never really knew her.

The thought came as a shock. His mind went to his mother's ring now safely hidden back inside the mining shack. Allie didn't seem like a real person anymore. At least not the Allie he knew. Had he really thought to marry her? What could have happened to change her?

Or maybe the girl I grew up with never truly existed.

None of that mattered anymore. Whatever had happened back there, whatever her reasons, he still had to escape. The ranch lay north and west. Before he could return he needed to lead them away from there. If this trail held he might be able to cut across the mountains and drop down toward Sheridan. He wasn't very familiar with that country, but the men from town wouldn't be either. He could lose any pursuit and circle back around to the mine. Then he could decide what to do next.

Forty thousand in gold. With that he could give Davis Judd a real fight.

10

Wanting an early start, Brett broke camp a couple hours before dawn. Once the sun was up he found a vantage point where he could watch over his backtrail to see if he'd gotten away clean. Two hours later his patience was rewarded when he spotted two men riding up through the trees. They were leaned over in the saddle, studying his backtrail.

He suspected both were Judd men. He recognized neither.

His first thought was to wait until they drew closer and then fire down at them. Odds were good he could kill them both. Once they passed through the trees they would have to cross a span of rocky open ground with nowhere to hide. There would be other men out hunting him though, and any gunfire would echo for miles. If he fired now, by noon the mountains would be crawling with men and —even if they didn't find him—they might stumble across the mine.

Was Mourning Song still there? He hadn't seen her yesterday when he rode out for Youngston. And what of Red Elk?

He doubted they would ever find the Crow. Red Elk seemed to have a knack for avoiding traps.

The best course for now is to lead this pair on away. They aren't sure of my trail or they'd have more men. He walked back to his horse and put his rifle back in its scabbard.

Then Brett mounted up and continued north toward Montana. He branched off the game trail crossing over the Bighorns to their eastern slope. The mountains were smaller as he moved north, worn down nubs compared to their strutting southern brothers. He broke a couple of green branches on a juniper where he left the trail—he didn't want to lose his pursuit completely—just to draw them off from any other searchers.

He thought about the two men behind him. *How much food did they have? None...most likely.* No doubt they believed they'd catch him quickly. He doubted they even had winter coats and while the warming spring held the valleys tight, up here in the mountains the cold was never more than a stray storm away. Growing up here, Brett had seen snow fly as late as June and as early as September on the taller peaks. They weren't so high this far north of course, but at night the temperature would still drop to near freezing.

Weaving down through the tree line, a shot shattered the bark of a pine just inches from his mare's nose. Brett spurred his horse and swung her down into the thicker screen of trees.

More shots rang out from above. None close this time.

They had surprised him. They were much closer than he'd thought. *Lucky they didn't kill me.* His hands shook and his mouth was dry. He'd never been hunted before. Not even when Kip Lane and his men shot him had he felt like this.

He did not like it. He wasn't some animal to be stalked, hunted down, and then killed.

Well, the elk have hooves and antlers to fight off their enemies. And I have weapons of my own.

Brett slid his rifle from its scabbard and dismounted. He tied his horse off to a stunted tree and started back up the trail. He squatted down behind a huge fallen log and peered through the maze of tree trunks.

He didn't have to wait long. In minutes a pair of horses galloped up the trail. Brett fired twice, putting the shots purposefully low. He wasn't a dry gulcher even though these men were. This wasn't like those guards hauling the Indian women, they might be simple towns-folk for all he knew; he didn't want to shoot an unwary man from cover.

A foolish notion, he chided himself. *There is no honor in matters like this. Respect between hunter and hunted is a lie.*

The pair scrambled off the trail. One practically fell off his horse.

"Why are you following me?" Brett yelled.

A smattering of shots struck the tree to his left. Brett fired twice in response and heard the wet smack of a bullet and then a man's painful grunt.

"Get him Jack," a voice wheezed.

"You both work for Davis Judd?" Brett said.

"What's it to you?"

"Davis Judd is a lying snake and a red-handed thief."

"Says a man who molested a woman," the man said.

"I molested no one," Brett said.

"If you knew who that girl belonged to you'd surrender now."

"And who's that?"

"Kip Lane, the gunfighter, and he sent us out after you."

"So you work for Lane then?" Brett asked. "He's a bushwhacker and a coyote."

A shot came from a low bush. Brett put three rounds into it. The bush yelped and a man stood up and swore. He clutched his arm near the elbow; his shirt was stained crimson.

A mistake friend. Brett shot him twice more in the chest.

He waited a few minutes for either man to move. The first man he'd shot started to groan again, and Brett slipped back away to his waiting horse.

Mounting up quickly, he took the reins and led the mare onward through the trees. Satisfied he was well clear, he swung west and climbed back up and over the worn spine of the mountains, and then swung south along the western slopes.

Travel was slow, the terrain rough and uneven. The day grew late, the shadows stretched and the sky held the first hints of bronze.

Brett found a quiet spot near an old deadfall that would screen his campfire. After cooking a few strips of salted pork he studied the slender flames. Over and over, he practiced drawing the Colt. He practiced mainly with his left hand, but sometimes he drew the spare pistol from behind his back with his right. Using his right certainly wasn't fast, painfully slow in fact. He'd never beat anyone to the draw that way; he wanted to have a feel for it though. The last thing he could afford was to fumble or drop the second gun if he needed it.

His mind wandered as he went back to practicing with his left.

I left two men to die in the brush today. How far have I come from that frightened boy falling down into the deep dark?

He wondered though what manner of man climbed out of that cold muddy grave. *Maybe Brett Rawlins truly died down there and I'm really am the ghost that took his place.* His mind went over recent events. So much had happened, but above all one word lodged in his thoughts.

Weak.

First Mourning Song and then Allie had called him that. He didn't feel weak. He knew he was reasonably skilled with his gun, and he'd proven willing to do use it. Four men that raised their hands against him were dead now. The loudmouth in Sheridan, Curly Red, the harmonica man, at least one on his trail just now. Four men dead. That didn't sound weak.

He wondered if the rest of the searchers had given up by now. He didn't have much food and the mine was miles away to the south. His father's cabin lay closer. Judd's second gunman, Seth Nelson, would be there. Like his boss the man was a thief. A thief, who ate at his parent's table, warmed himself by their stove, even slept in their bed.

The Colt appeared in his left hand. Brett squeezed the grip until it hurt. Seth Nelson, a known gunfighter, stood between him and his father's ranch. Tomorrow he'd find out just how fast he really was.

———

BRETT LAY FACE down in a clump of ancient sage watching the front door of his father's cabin.

The morning had grown late now; the sun shone high and bright, and he'd left his canteen on his horse. There had been no reason to bring it. He didn't plan on lying here all morning. Only, he didn't expect Nelson to sleep in for so long. A bead of sweat ran down his nose and hung there until he wiped it away.

His plan was simple. He wasn't going to give Nelson an even chance. This wasn't about pride or seeing who was faster; this was about taking back his father's home.

Brett didn't want to barge into the cabin, guns blazing. Though he knew the inside well, he couldn't be sure exactly where Nelson might be. So instead he'd wait outside for Nelson to reveal himself, and then he could circle around the cabin or sneak in behind the barn and get the drop on him.

Trying not to think about how dry his mouth was, Brett listened to a bee drifting from flower to flower. A rabbit hopped beneath the sagebrush just ahead of him. A few cotton-white clouds passed overhead but the shady relief they offered was fleeting.

Finally, when Brett was moments from crawling back to his canteen, the front door banged open roughly and Nelson emerged. The gunman was dressed for riding, spurs and fringed leather chaps, and he headed straightaway for the corrals.

Damn it all. The plan was to catch Nelson off guard not chase him over half the country. *I should have waited for evening when he sits on the porch.*

He'd been so focused on getting the job done he hadn't considered what would happen if Nelson just come out and rode off.

Some instinct ticked at the back of Brett's thoughts. *I could let Nelson ride off and just wait for him to return. That might be the safest course.*

The gunman came back into view leading a magnificent red stallion. *Cimarron*, Jim Rawlins' pride and joy. Nelson swung up into the saddle, rolled a cigarette, and lit it. Briefly his eyes swept over Brett's concealment; then he spurred Cimarron and headed downhill behind the cabin and passed out of view.

Brett swore. With the appearance of Cimarron all thoughts of waiting were banished. He couldn't allow this gunman to ride his father's horse. He scrambled back to his own horse and hopped into the saddle. Still this could work. He had an advantage. He knew the trails around the ranch better than Nelson. He'd played all over these hills from the time he could walk.

Nelson took the trail toward Clear Lake, a spring-fed patch of water to the southwest. The good news was that the trail was fairly straight, no danger of being caught on a switchback. The bad news was that it followed along a dry wash lined with gnarled old cottonwoods. Getting a clear shot would be nearly impossible.

For the better part of an hour Brett followed the gunman. Nelson set a quick pace, too quick for Brett to use any of the other trails he knew to circle around and cut him off. He glimpsed Nelson in short, windowed gaps between the fluttering cottonwood leaves. He smelled the dust raised from Cimarron's hooves.

Brett swung around a little crook in the trail and suddenly realized Nelson's tracks were gone. He froze. He looked in the trees, along the road, and then toward the open plain.

Where did he go? He suddenly felt very exposed. A sickening knot of fear formed in his stomach.

"Hello," a hard voice said from behind him. "I don't believe we've met."

Brett itched to draw his gun, but forced himself not to move. Nelson had him dead to rights. The instant he started for the Colt Nelson would kill him. His mind raced. How could he escape?

"We haven't," Brett said. "I was hoping to hire you for a job."

"Hire me?" Nelson chuckled a little. "Well then I guess I'm a little confused."

"Confused?"

"You laid up in the brush all morning watching over my house. I spend every evening sitting on my porch studying that ridge you hid on so I spotted you right off. And then you followed me out here. I set a pace you could catch, but you kept back out of sight the whole time. A suspicious man might think you were planning to kill me."

Brett kept his hands still and slowly turned his horse with just his knees. He gave Nelson an appraising look. The gunfighter spoke with a hint of an accent. Irish maybe. Nelson's gun was still in its holster; unlike Kip Lane he wore just the one.

"Needed to see if you were as good as advertised," Brett said.

"Did you now?" Nelson squinted. "Well most people—those interested in hiring me—want to know about how fast I am." In a flash the gun sprang into his hand. He pointed it casually at Brett. "They don't bother to see if I can catch someone following me."

"Of course," Nelson went on, "it isn't all about speed."

"It's not?" Brett asked.

"No." Shaking his head a little, Nelson gave him a half-smile. "It doesn't really matter how fast you are if you can't hit what you aim at. I've seen men draw like lighting itself only to put their first three shots down in the dirt. One of them shot his own boot in fact. Took his big toe clean off. And then there's the hang-ups."

"Hang-ups?"

"Sure. Take your gun there," Nelson nodded to the Colt. "The front sight. You haven't filed it smooth. Now and then it will hang up when you draw."

Brett looked down at the Colt as if seeing it for the first time. He had noticed the front sight hanging at times, but he'd learned to work around it by angling the Colt's grip forward and powering through it with his arm.

"I know what you're thinking. You're thinking you can tilt the grip a little forward when you draw and it will still clear. See that works but it slows down the draw and, more importantly, once the gun is out you have to bring it further up toward your target. Takes extra time."

Nelson holstered his gun then quickly drew it again.

"See," his smile was wide now, teeth white. "Comes out smooth and level and ready to shoot. Now, let's talk about that job you had for me."

Brett licked his lips. *He knows I'm lying. Any minute now he'll call me on it and start shooting. I have to gamble.* Instead of answering he let out an ear-splitting whistle.

Cimarron's ears perked and the big stallion exploded like a tornado, bucking and kicking and whipping around in a circle. Nelson squeezed off a single wild shot, missing Brett by a mile. Then his gun fell when he grabbed at the pommel with both hands and desperately tried to hold on.

The red stallion threw his great head down, bucked forward kicking with both hind feet, then whipped his head back up viciously. A hit like that would kill a man.

To his credit Nelson saw the blow coming and let go the pommel like it was red hot; he left the saddle flying. Brett slapped spurs to his horse and shot up the trail for the cover of the cottonwoods. He whistled again, a low warbling note this time, and Cimarron abruptly stopped bucking and galloped after him.

Both horses were off and running then. Hooves pounding in rhythm with Brett's hammering heart. He waited until they were well away from where Nelson fell and then he leaned to Cimarron and scooped up the big horse's reins.

"Good. Good boy," Brett said as he patted Cimarron's powerful neck. "I sure missed you big fella."

He led the red horse toward the mine shack. He avoided his father's cabin; he didn't need to push his luck even a hair further today. He'd been lucky, damned lucky, to survive his encounter with Seth Nelson. His face flushed with shame. Nelson could have killed him at any time.

I've been a fool. What was I thinking trailing after him like that? The man is a proven gunfighter and I'm just a...what exactly? Brett could only shake his head. *A fool and certainly no gunman.*

Davis Judd, Kip Lane, Seth Nelson, he had to stop taking these men lightly. He had to treat them with respect and be willing to fight them as ruthlessly as they would him. To beat these men he needed to become one of them.

11

When Brett returned to the mine, Red Elk was waiting. The Crow stood beneath the little shack's wooden awning, face impassive as a statue, studying the clouds.

Brett unsaddled his mare and then Cimarron before turning both out in the little corral. With all the horses he was gathering they needed more space. There was a grassy meadow to the north. Plenty of open area. Forming a steep rocky wall, the mountain lifted up over the eastern side of the meadow and, by fencing off the rest, he could enclose another five acres with only a little work.

Tomorrow, I'll start cutting logs into posts and rails.

Saddle in hand, he approached Red Elk on the little porch. "You found me." Brett said unsurprised.

"I said I would." Red Elk shifted his feet uncomfortably. "The woman is inside. She has prepared a meal."

The woman? Mourning Song. Brett had almost forgotten about her. She must have been here alone the last few days while he'd been away. Why hadn't she left after the other night?

"How'd you get her to go inside?"

Red Elk shrugged. "She was there when I arrived."

Brett followed Red Elk inside.

Morning Song waited for them there. When they entered she sprang to their feet. She'd placed several skins on the floor, arranging them in the same manner as they had been in her grandfather's teepee. The chair and table were pushed away against the far wall. There was a fire in the stove and the smell of food caused Brett's stomach to rumble.

Red Elk took a seat with his back to the door and Brett sat down opposite him.

Mourning Song took up a piece of thick leather with several cuts of meat arranged on it. Beside the meat were three small loaves of coarsely ground bread. *Probably some of the horse's corn*, Brett decided. She served the food and then poured water into a pair of battered tin cups. Then she knelt at Brett's left. She squatted on her knees waiting until he and Red Elk were done eating, then she took what was left for herself.

From time to time, Brett glanced at her while she ate. Last night she'd been so angry and all over nothing. A simple cup of coffee.

There was no trace of that biting anger on her features now. She sat serene and calm, composed like she was attending church. A strange woman. Nothing at all like the gentle Lisa Sweeney.

When he'd seen her last, Lisa had been all smiles and laughter and joy. He'd told her his plans after he took the ranch back and she'd listened with rapt interest. In an odd way, Lisa was more like an innocent child than a grown woman.

Mourning Song caught him studying her. She raised her chin and slanted her eyes at him. Cool and composed, she continued to eat.

Nothing childlike about her.

"What will you do next?" Red Elk said.

"I don't know."

Brett rose and walked out to the porch to watch the setting sun.

It seemed like everything he tried so far had failed miserably. He'd gone off to kill Kip Lane and instead gotten himself pursued by a posse. Then he'd tried to take Seth Nelson out of the fight and that disaster had almost gotten him killed.

Maybe Gideon Sweeney is right. Maybe I should just cut my losses and move on.

He had money now, a little at least. The reward for Curly Red and what he'd taken from Davis Judd would last him for a good long while. He could live easy for a time and if he decided to ride west he could catch on with a cattle outfit. He had the skills certainly. He was a good cowhand, his father had seen to it.

But that wouldn't get his father's ranch back. And it wasn't enough to start his own place. Not nearly.

He wished he had someone to talk to, someone to ask about his problem. For all his wisdom, Gideon Sweeney seemed to have few real ideas. He had problems of his own. His plan to appeal to the Governor had gained him nothing.

Brett sighed. He ran his fingers through his hair. His father would know what to do. Jim Rawlins never had a moment of self-doubt.

As he stood watching the day's last golden rays, he gained the first inkling of an idea on what to try next. If he couldn't beat Davis Judd head-on there were other ways to hurt him. If Allie hadn't been lying, there was still the shipment of gold she had told him about. He had some time before it arrived. But he had another idea as well. Something he could start tomorrow.

"Thank you for the meal," Brett said to Mourning Song. She gave him a questioning look. *Maybe her English isn't as good as I thought.* He turned to Red Elk. "Will you tell her thanks for me?"

Red Elk hesitated for a moment then translated. She looked first at the Crow and then her eyes shifted to him. Her face colored crimson. She rose suddenly, jammering something that he didn't understand. She snatched up what was left of the food, threw it on the table, and then stomped outside.

"What just happened?" Brett asked. "Did you translate what I said? What did she say?"

Red Elk only watched after her for a time. "All women are crazy," he said. "None more so than that one."

———

THEY BEGAN BRANDING cattle the following day.

For the past few months Judd's men had been hard at work branding over the Rawlins 4L into a 9O and—with a red hot cinch ring—Brett covered it again, this time with an 88. Brett grinned at the sight of the first cow wearing her new brand.

Davis Judd won't much care for that.

Brett was careful to steal back only his own cattle; he knew them well enough to pick them out. If he was caught and Judd decided to argue the brand they could skin the cow and show that Judd himself had worked over the Rawlins original. Every lawman in Wyoming would be after him if he were caught rustling.

With Red Elk and Mourning Song's help, he pushed each of the rebranded cattle, one after another, up into a narrow box canyon. Before they started, Brett had fenced off the entrance with cut aspen poles where they couldn't stray. He wanted to hurt Judd. He also wanted more money to hire gunmen of his own. With winter now gone, he could drive the little herd over the mountains down into Sheridan and sell them there.

Day-by-day they worked. Sunup to sundown. The process was slow. Mourning Song and Red Elk fought the brush to bring the cattle to him, both were excellent riders, while he branded them over.

Mourning Song repeated her dinner each night. The food was always good. She could cook, Brett granted. After what had happened earlier, he wasn't sure if he should thank her or not so he kept quiet about it. *No need for a repeat of that first night.* He brewed his own coffee and Red Elk quickly grew to like it.

Mourning Song wouldn't touch hers. She only wrinkled her nose and stared suspiciously at the boiling pot.

One night, after a particularly hard day, they camped outside the stuffy little cabin and after they finished their meal Mourning Song rose. She lifted her arms, spread them slowly to either side. With the pale moonlight crowning her hair and the cookfire's orange glow glazing her tanned features, she looked like an ancient goddess holding up a blanket of stars. Slowly, she began to dance. She spun first her arms and then each leg in delicate arches. She shuffled her feet and swayed her hips wide to her own rhythm, moving in little whirls and turns. Her breathing was deep and even. She was beautiful and free and—in that moment—completely lost to her own inner music. Dark smoldering fire played in her obsidian eyes. She did not smile, she didn't speak, but her lips were full and parted. She moved with a natural grace.

Brett felt his blood boil just to look at her. He could only watch. He wasn't sure he'd even breathed the whole time.

When she was finished, she caught Brett staring at her. She gave him a flat look, neither pleased nor angry. Then she lowered her arms and retreated back to her blankets.

"A strange woman," Brett said.

"Beautiful though," Red Elk agreed.

"Very," Brett licked his dry lips. "Was that a special dance?"

"Among the Crow we have many dances. Some for celebration, some for loss, some for great happiness."

"And that one?"

"That is one for courting."

"Courting?" Brett said. *Why would she dance like that up here with us?* He poked a stick into the fire stirring the glowing embers. "Maybe it means something else for the Cheyenne."

Red Elk only looked at him.

When they had fifty head rebranded, Brett opened the gate and started the little herd out over the mountain toward Sheridan. He could have gathered more, there were certainly enough cows running loose on the ranch, but they'd been lucky to go undiscovered by the Davis riders and working with smaller groups would be safer.

Brett rode Cimarron almost exclusively now. The big red stallion was the best cattle horse he'd ever seen. He was surefooted as a mountain goat and had both speed and endurance to spare. He and Brett did the harder job, pushing the cattle from the rear, while Red Elk and Mourning Song directed the herd from either flank.

Like the cattle, Brett's thoughts kept straying as they rode. Every day he'd expected to find some sign that a Judd rider had learned of the shack, but so far nothing. It didn't make sense. A great many of the man's cattle were scattered on the range, but now that the rebranding was done there were no cowboys watching them. It didn't make sense.

Where is he keeping all his men? And more importantly what are they doing?

The gold. Of course Davis would have several watching the incoming gold shipment. Some would be on his home place. Likely rebuilding his house. Still he should have had a few men watching his herd. There were wolves and bears and mountain lions in the Bighorns and the cattle needed to be protected.

Where are the cowboys who are supposed to be watching the herd?

Unable to answer the question, Brett concentrated on driving the cattle. After a time Red Elk dropped back to ride beside him.

"I know of a place ahead, a big meadow, just over the pass. It is off the main trail and out of sight," the Crow said.

"Sounds good. I don't want to meet anyone if we can avoid it," Brett said.

It took the better part of a day to reach the place, and it proved everything Red Elk said and more. Centered around a little creek, the meadow covered at least twenty acres. A wildfire must have cleared it a few years ago as there were tall black tree stumps scattered throughout. The grass was excellent, lush and a deep healthy green, almost a foot in height. The cattle took to it eagerly.

Brett decided to let them linger a full day to take advantage of the meadow. The horses could certainly use the rest as well. Their supplies were low so in the morning he and Red Elk set out hunting. They found sign of a few deer and an elk but never saw anything close enough to shoot at.

The day was almost gone, and they met on the trail back to camp.

"No luck?" Brett asked. He couldn't see any bundles of meat on the Crow's horse.

"No. Not even any fresh tracks."

"Some hunters we are. Mourning Song will be awfully—" Brett's thoughts were cutoff by a gunshot. "That came from the camp," he said.

He touched Cimarron with his spurs and the big red horse tore off toward the sound.

The ground was wet with snowmelt and, as Cimarron's hooves ate up the distance, black clods flew with every step. Brett leaned low in the saddle. He squeezed his eyes shut as the wind and the stallion's wild flying mane whipped at him.

Soon they topped out over a little rise and were passing into thick trees. Trusting Cimarron's judgment better than his own, Brett let the stallion have its head. Through the blurring screen of tree trunks the green meadow gradually came into sight. Like a red cannonball, he and the big horse exploded into the clearing. The cattle were spooked —he saw that right off—their heads lifted and ears alert. They were all gathered back on the near side of the meadow watching across to the opposite end.

Another shot and they'll bolt for sure.

He slowed Cimarron a little and palmed his Colt.

He looked all around for Mourning Song. At first, he didn't see her. Then he spotted her at the meadow's very edge, hunched down over a mound of shaggy brown fur. She didn't appear to be injured, but there was fresh blood on her hands up to the elbows.

She's hurt.

Brett felt his breath catch. Mourning Song straightened; in one hand she held an antler-handled knife and in the other a long strip of bloody meat.

She looked up when she heard him and smiled. Odd. He never would have expected that. She held up the strip for him to see and over her shoulder he saw the huge head of a mountain lion.

Brett jumped down beside her.

"Are you hurt? Are you alright?"

Her expression changed to one of confusion. She said something he didn't understand.

Brett took her by the shoulders. "Are you hurt?"

"No." She shook her head.

"No?" It took a moment for Brett to understand. She'd spoken; more than that she answered him.

His eyes roamed over her and he stepped around her to check her back. There were a few scattered drops of blood but no wounds. Most of the blood was limited to her arms. He moved to the lion then. There was a single bullet hole, dead center in the lion's breast.

Heart shot, thing never knew what hit it.

A rifle lay in the grass beside the lion.

"She is a good shot," Red Elk said as he joined them. "But I am surprised you let her have a rifle."

Mourning Song spoke to him in her own language, gestured with the strip of meat—there were several already carved out of the lion's flank—picked up the rifle, and started back toward camp.

"I didn't. She must have snuck it out after we left." Brett watched her go. He recognized the rifle of course. It was his old single-shot hunting gun. The one he'd left in the shack.

"Lucky she hasn't shot you yet then."

"What did she say?"

"She asked if you were angry with her."

"Why would I be?"

"In most tribes women are forbidden to hunt," the Crow said. He didn't volunteer whether or not that included his own people.

"I am not of her tribe. I was only worried she was hurt," Brett said. He thought for a moment. "Why would she care if I was angry?"

Red Elk smiled.

"And when did she learn what 'no' means?"

"I've been teaching her a few words. She knew some from Watches Deer," Red Elk said. He grinned. "Isn't 'no' the first word a woman should learn?"

For the first time in a long time, whether from relief or humor, Brett threw back his head and laughed. He couldn't remember the last time he'd really laughed. It felt good and he barely recognized the sound of it. "That sounds like something my father would say."

12

It took two more days for the little trail drive to reach Sheridan.

On the south side of town were a number of stock pens. Brett, Red Elk, and Mourning Song drove the cattle straight there and penned them easy enough. Though its industry was turning more to a coal, Sheridan had deep roots as a cowtown. From spring on through summer buyers would drift into town to purchase local cattle, and then in bigger herds drive them to market at the railhead down in Cheyenne.

Once the gate was closed a local cowboy approached him.

"What outfit you with?"

"Rawlins from over the mountain."

"You're a little early."

"I need the money."

"Don't we all," the cowboy smiled. "Odd looking brand."

"Jim Rawlins, my father, was a known man in these parts. He sold here occasionally. He ran a 4L, but I wanted something of my own. Easy enough to switch them over."

"Easy to switch a lot of things over to a double eight. Not that I'm implying anything," the cowboy gave him a half-grin.

"Any buyers in town?" Brett asked.

"Mitch Stephens, Bill Hollis, a few others. Stick around and I'm sure they'll come out of the woodwork to find you. Anywhere in particular I should send 'em?"

"I'm Brett Rawlins, and I'll be at the hotel." He knew Bill Hollis— not well—but he'd come by the ranch several times to speak with his father and wound up either buying or selling a few head. According to the elder Rawlins, Hollis had been honest and fair in his dealings.

A rare thing these days.

The cowhand shifted his eyes off behind Brett. "Your hands might not be welcome in town."

Brett followed his gaze to Red Elk and Mourning Song. The Indians looked back impassively. There were other cowboys starting to gather around, several were pointing at the pair and talking low among themselves. "Well then tell the buyers I'll be camped just south of town."

"Will do," the cowboy nodded.

Brett rode over to Red Elk. "We'll camp south of town. Either of you need anything from the store before we go?"

"No," Red Elk said. He eyed the crowd and spoke to Mourning Song in Cheyenne. She said something back and he translated. "She wishes to go with you."

"Alright," Brett agreed. "But I might need you to translate."

"I do not think that would be wise," he looked again over the crowd. "I will find us a good camp."

With that the Crow started out and left him alone with Mourning Song. The crowd watched Red Elk go, and Brett sensed their growing relief. For now at least, they seemed to notice Mourning Song less than the warrior.

Maybe they think she's the less dangerous of the two. Remembering the way she'd waved her knife at him, Brett snorted. Of the two he'd face Red Elk a dozen times before crossing Mourning Song. *Well what the people of Sheridan don't know won't hurt them.*

Brett took advantage of the distraction Red Elk's leaving was making, and led Mourning Song off to the general store.

He helped her down from her horse, and she followed him inside.

The storekeeper gave him a hopeful look, but that slipped a notch when he saw Mourning Song. He started to speak. Brett cut him off. "It's alright. She's with me. We won't be long. Just looking for a few supplies." He flashed one of Davis Judd's gold coins and the storekeeper licked his lips and relaxed a bit.

Brett picked up several boxes of ammunition then bought a few pounds of flour, salt, sugar, cured bacon, coffee—Mourning Song frowned at that—and a new repeating rifle. The storekeeper's eyes brightened as Brett counted out the money.

While he paid the bill, Mourning Song ran her hands over a bundle of dark blue cloth with small yellow sunflowers printed on it.

"How much for a few yards of that?" Brett nodded to the cloth.

"A bit per yard," the man said.

"I'll take six yards then. I want needles and some blue thread to match as well." He counted out a few more coins.

The storekeeper measured out the fabric, cut it, and handed it to Brett.

"For you," Brett said as he passed the material to Mourning Song.

She took the cloth and nodded, then clutched it to her chest like it was the most precious thing in the world.

Once the supplies were loaded they followed after Red Elk and found his camp near a little creek. The Crow had killed a deer the day before and he had a haunch on a long skewer over the fire.

"You got coffee?" he asked.

Brett nodded. "And these for you." He handed the Crow a box of ammunition for the big Sharps.

Red Elk smiled as he took the box and dumped the shells into his leather pouch. "With these I will kill many white men."

"Just make sure it's the right ones," Brett answered. He handed the new rifle to Mourning Song and her eyes lit up. "Does she know how to use this?"

Red Elk repeated the question in Cheyenne. In answer she loaded the rifle with a few shells and cycled the breech to put a round in the chamber. She then squeezed the trigger while lowering the hammer with her thumb.

"It would seem so," Red Elk said.

With that they settled down to dinner.

"How much are your cows worth?" the Crow asked once the meal was done.

"Maybe twenty-five dollars a head," Brett considered for a moment. "I could do a little better if we drove them closer to the rails but it would take longer."

"I would like to buy some from you."

"Ohh?"

"Not from this group. But later."

"What for?"

"My people would start their own herds. The government does not always give us enough food to get through the winter. If we had cattle of our own we could change that. Would you sell some of your cows to us?"

"You'll want young stock then, breeding age." The kind of stock Brett needed to keep his own ranch going. Red Elk had saved Brett's life though and had shown himself loyal time and again. He'd worked to help Brett and asked nothing in return.

More than that he is a friend and I've precious few of those.

"I won't sell you any," Brett started. "But by way of thanks for your help I will give you a few head, young stock to start your herd, and also some older cows and bulls to feed your people through the immediate winter."

Seeming satisfied, Red Elk nodded. "A man comes," he said. "I will care for the horses." He took Cimarron and Mourning Song's palomino and led them away from the fire.

Brett looked toward Sheridan seeing nothing at first. Then out of the dark a single rider appeared.

He raised a hand as he drew up and called out, "Howdy. Looking for the Rawlins outfit."

"You found them," Brett said. "Come on down Mr. Hollis."

Hollis froze for a minute, then grinned, and swung on down. "Brett Rawlins," he shook his head. "Jim's son from over in Pryor. I didn't put it together until just now. Must have been that shiny new brand that threw me. Double Eight? When did that happen?"

"When Davis Judd decided to brand over the 4L into a 90." Brett shook the cattle buyer's hand.

"Ahh, and you returned the favor." Bill Hollis grinned. "Well your father's like that. Damn cagey that Jim Rawlins."

For a moment Brett wasn't sure what to say. Normally his father's death didn't bother him—he tried not to even think of it—but for some reason it hit him hard tonight. He swallowed and started in. "Pa's gone actually. He passed last year. I buried him beside mother on the little knoll near the cabin."

Bill's face fell. "How'd that happen?"

"He hung himself."

"Jim Rawlins? You're sure lad?"

"I am."

Hollis studied the ground. "I just can't believe that. Your father was the toughest man I ever knew. He'd never do something like that."

"He wasn't the same man after Ma died."

"I'm sorry to hear that. He sure loved your ma and missed her something fierce, but I hoped he'd pull out of it."

Brett waited a minute before going on. He wasn't sure why he'd told the buyer the truth. Only he was suddenly tired of carrying the weight of it all around on his own. "I told Sheriff Payson he'd gotten caught in a blizzard. Didn't want anyone thinking less of him."

"I understand," Bill nodded. "That's good of you. You're a good lad Brett."

"Bill, you've seen my herd. It's all we could gather up and drive over quickly. How much are they worth?"

"Wrong time of year to sell. Autumn or late summer would be better."

"Davis Judd, a newcomer, has a couple of gunhands holding father's ranch. I've tried taking it back, but there's little I can do. I'm no gunman. I figured if I can't fight him off I could at least bring a few head over the mountain and sell them."

"You stole these cows?"

"Just stealing back what's mine. I thought if I made enough money I could hire a gunhand or two of my own."

"That's not a very good idea," Hollis shifted uncomfortably. "It costs a lot to pay a good one and even more to keep him. Besides, right now most every gunman in Wyoming is all tied up in what folks are calling the Johnson County War."

"What else can I do? Sheriff Payson is gone. Judd's got one of his own men for Sheriff now. I need to push him out of father's ranch somehow."

"And you think stealing his cattle will work?"

"I think it's the only choice I have," Brett snapped. He knew it wasn't much of a plan, but he couldn't come up with anything else. "I took care to only steal back my own cows. You can kill one and peel back the hide if it makes you feel better."

Hollis raised his hands defensively. "No need for that lad. Just trying to understand the lay of the land here."

"Now how much are they worth?"

"I can give you twenty-two a head for them. That's the best I can do."

"Deal."

"I can't pay you tonight. Come by the hotel in the morning."

"I'll be there early," Brett shook his hand.

After the cattle buyer left and they'd settled down for the night, Brett looked into the fire.

Those cattle would have sold for thirty a piece in the fall. *But I need the cash now if I'm going to hire enough men to run Davis Judd off father's ranch.*

Men weren't cheap. Fighting men especially. *Can I even find any? No doubt Bill has the right of it.* Every man capable of fighting would be taking sides in the Powder River country.

What am I going to do now?

————

BRETT WATCHED Red Elk and Mourning Song ride out just before dawn while he went back into Sheridan to meet up with Bill Hollis. They would return to the ranch and start gathering more cattle to drive up north to the Crow reservation in Montana while he finished his sale.

He arrived at the hotel as they were serving breakfast; a pair of waitresses worked table to table like a pair of honeybees busy gathering pollen. Ordering only coffee, Brett settled into a table to wait for the cattle buyer. He didn't have to wait long.

"Brett," Hollis said as he shook his hand. The buyers face was solemn, his eyes held a haunted look. He handed over a signed bank note. "You can cash this either in Pryor or here in town. I honestly feel terrible about the price. At least let me buy you breakfast."

Their waitress, a young woman with white-blonde hair, served them each a plate piled high with eggs, bacon, sliced cheese, and steaming bread.

"I still can't believe that about your father," Hollis said. He met Brett's eyes. "Hanging himself? That's just not like the Jim Rawlins I knew."

"I found him myself," Brett said uncomfortably. This was the last thing he wanted to talk about this morning. "You know where I can hire a few men to help me?"

"Gunhands?"

"If I can afford them," Brett nodded.

"Sorry, but no. Last week there were a couple staying here in Sheridan, but they pulled stakes for Cheyenne."

Brett could only shake his head in disgust. He'd been a fool. Again. *Maybe the best thing is to just pull my own stakes and head out.* The last time he'd spoken with Gideon Sweeney it sounded like the Mormons were reaching the same decision.

"Brett, as your friend and a friend to your father, I've got to tell you. I spoke with a couple of other buyers and stockmen from down south last night. Davis Judd has been invited to join the Cattleman's Association. That's the group stirring up all the trouble with the squatters down in the Powder Basin."

"What are you saying?"

"I'm saying this Davis Judd has powerful friends. The Governor looks favorably on the Association. You could wind up with a lot more enemies than you know. In fact, the Association is meeting here in town. I've seen a couple members here in the hotel."

"What would you have me do Bill? Let him take what my parents worked all their lives for?" Brett's voice rose. A pair of men at the next table gave him a wary look, and he fought down his temper. He did not need to draw attention.

"Are you sure you want to go through with all of this?" Hollis asked. "I'm only saying I don't think your parents would want you risking your life for a few acres of rocky ground. Fighting this Davis Judd character is bucking a stacked deck."

"I've got to be going," Brett said as he stood. First Sweeney and now Hollis. He was sick of everyone telling him to let just his father's ranch go.

No, it's more than just a ranch it was father's dream. And I can't let it die can I?

"Well, if I can't talk you out of it then I wish you the best of luck," Bill said.

"Thanks Bill, I appreciate it." Brett started out and noticed a group of men in dark, tailored suits gathered in a smaller room off to one side. Some smoked cigars or read papers as others spoke amongst themselves. While he was looking the wrong direction, he bumped into a big man on his way in to join them.

"Watch where you're going," the big man rumbled.

Brett turned to him. He started to apologize. "Sorry I—"

"Well well, if it isn't young Brett Rawlins," a second man said. "Why just the other day I heard you were no longer with us."

Brett knew the voice immediately. His hand started of its own volition and then he remembered he'd left the leather thong on his Colt.

"Now there, Mr. Rawlins. No need for that," Judd Davis said. He eyed Brett but didn't seem worried in the slightest. In fact he wore one of his little wolf-smiles.

The other man, the one Brett had bumped, stepped up between them.

"I don't believe you've met my foreman, John Hollande. John handles my cattle for me. Odd that we've run into you here. John was just telling me about a rather interesting brand he saw down in the sale pens. What was it John?"

"An Eighty-Eight, a rustler's brand if ever there was one," the big man growled.

Brett froze. Here was Davis Judd and he had his gun, only the thong held it in place and he'd never get it drawn before the rancher's foreman reached him.

John Hollande threw him a dark grin as if he knew what Brett was thinking. He was a bruiser of a man, well over six feet tall, powerfully built in the neck and shoulders and chest, with greying hair but a young square-jawed face. His crooked nose had been broken at least once, and his eyes were small and deep set.

"You've rendered him speechless John," Judd said.

"Rustler's brand?" Brett coughed. "I'd say that Nine-Ohh you're running is the rustler's brand. We could always kill one of those steers to skin him and see just what the original brand was."

Hollande gave a little growl.

"My money's on a 4L," Brett finished.

"Watch your tongue boy," Hollande said.

"I'm talking to your boss not you." Brett gave him a sideways look. "How about it Judd? Or maybe I should tell your friends in there all about how you stole your ranch? About how you're just another Johnny-come-lately squatter. From what I've heard they don't much care for squatters. That'd make a good tale."

The room was silent all around them. Brett felt every eye on them, but he kept his full attention on Davis. The man wasn't smiling now. His eyes held a deep hate.

"You're the squatter," Davis muttered.

"My father settled that land when there was nothing out here but Indians," Brett said loud enough for the room to hear. "He fought them along with the bears and lions and wolves. He came to this country before there was a Pryor or even a Sheridan and then we followed him out. He bought part of it off an old man who headed back to Billings."

"Bill Hollis," Brett nodded to the still seated cattle buyer. "He knows me and my father and all about the 4L. And these men know him. I'm sure he'll be happy to tell them all about Jim Rawlins. Or maybe we should settle this ourselves. Outside."

Judd's eyes narrowed. His face flushed red as he tried to keep his anger in check.

Brett's voice carried louder still. "You can always call me a liar."

Judd froze. He knew what such a challenge meant. The law wasn't here to settle this and, even if they were, they'd do nothing if Davis called him out.

For a second, Brett thought Judd would take him up on it. The look in Judd's eyes was pure venom. Bill Hollande interrupted though.

"This isn't the place," he muttered to his boss.

"Let him speak for himself," Brett said. "Surely a man like Davis Judd can speak for himself. He was loud enough when he called me a rustler. Louder still when he called me a squatter."

Judd's eyes bulged, and then something changed. He grew cold. He took a breath and seemed to relax.

Just then a pair of men wearing bronze stars fought their way through the crowd.

"What's all this?" the older man said. He carried a double-barreled shotgun and had it tilted in their direction.

"Not a thing Marshal," Davis said. "Just a friendly disagreement between neighbors."

"Well we don't want any friendly disagreements here in my peaceful little town." The Marshal moved a step closer squarely between Brett and Judd. "Now I know everyone in my county and that doesn't include either of you so why don't you both go your separate ways. If you've got a problem settle it back wherever you're from."

"C'mon boss," Hollande said. "There will be another time."

"Good day, young Mr. Rawlins," Davis said. With that he and John Hollande started for the door.

"Maybe I'll come visit your house again," Brett called after them. "Hopefully you'll be there next time."

Judd paused in the door like he'd been stabbed. For a moment Brett thought he'd turn to fight, but Hollande put a huge hand on his back and then they were gone.

Brett turned to go and found the Marshal was watching him. Still held loose near the Marshal's waist, the shotgun held an unspoken threat. Brett's eyes shifted from it to the Marshal then over his shoulder to a stunned Bill Hollis.

"Another time Bill," Brett said.

"It's been entertaining, Brett. You're every bit Jim Rawlins' son I'll give you that." He doffed his hat.

"Be on about your business son," the steel-eyed lawman said.

"Marshal." Brett tipped the brim of his hat then turned and was out the door.

When he got to the street he half-expected Davis Judd or John Hollande to be waiting for him but neither was in sight. He picked up Cimarron from the stables and rode out quickly. He wouldn't put it past either man to shoot him in the back.

Well if they didn't know I was alive before they certainly do now.

13

At a quick trot, Brett traveled north out of Sheridan. The pass they'd come across was almost due east, but he was worried Davis might have men following him. The last thing he wanted or needed was to lead them back to the mine.

There was a lesser-known crossing over the Bighorns that came out a ways north of Youngston and he rode straight for it. The trail was rugged, full of jagged rocks and switchbacks. Weaving through them, he had to take his time. Brett stopped just short of the highest point and settled down with his back against a stunted pine, watching his backtrail for almost an hour.

Nothing. *If Judd sent men I've already lost them, or they are far behind.*

He retrieved his horse and set out at a quick pace. Snow still clung to the peaks shouldering the pass, but the trail itself was clear. On the downward slope he swung north, instead of south toward home, and cut over into the wild country near the Montana border. He walked his horse through several streams, slowly turning west and then south until he'd made a wide circle. He crossed trails with a sheepherder and mingled his tracks with their flock's. According to

Red Elk, his trailcraft left much to be desired, but he was confident he'd hidden his route well enough.

North of the cabin was a little pool hidden at the foot of the mountain and surrounded by huge granite boulders. Brett turned Cimarron toward it. More than once, he'd snuck away from his chores to go swimming. After so many days on the trail, he needed a bath. He was already late; he'd told Red Elk to expect him before noon and it was now late afternoon.

But a little more late won't hurt. And I surely need a bath.

A maze of tree-sized boulders circled the pool like a herd of thirsty buffalo, and Brett tied Cimarron out where he could graze. He gave the horse a good scratching beneath his chin and made his way down toward the water, stripping off his shirt and leaving it on a big rock. He leaned down to feel the glassy water. Icy. He needn't have bothered; it was always cold. He started shucking off his pants and heard a noisy splash from across the pool.

Brett drew his gun and leaned out around a boulder where he could see more of the water.

Mourning Song—completely naked—was climbing out of the pool on the far bank. She sat on one of a flat, chair-sized rock, back toward him and started wringing water out of her long midnight hair.

Ashamed at seeing her, Brett started back but the gravel under his feet shifted, and she turned in time to see him.

Her eyes widened at first. Then she regarded him with a narrow dangerous look—not the usual fiery anger—but a smoldering gaze, something like the way she'd looked at him after her dance beneath the moonlight.

Brett froze. He felt his cheeks growing hot. He hadn't meant to startle her. He certainly hadn't meant to see her like that. He couldn't seem to tear himself free from her gaze though. Her eyes held him fast.

She is beautiful beyond words.

For a long time, Mourning Song only watched him; then she picked up her buckskins and held them over her breasts. Spell suddenly broken, Brett retreated where he couldn't see her. He waited for a long time and then slowly peered back around the boulder. She was gone, the flat rock still damp where she'd sat.

He started to put his shirt back on and decided he still needed the bath.

The icy water might do me good.

He skinned out of his pants and eased into the pool. He waded out until the water was up to his waist then swam deeper. He dipped below the surface, and then he turned back to the shore. He started out of the water when he saw Mourning Song—fully dressed in her buckskins now—watching him from beside his clothes.

"I didn't mean to see you like that," he said.

She grinned a little then picked up his pants and started back away from the pool.

"Hey now. I said I didn't mean to see you. Bring back my pants."

She paused to look at him, but he kept to the water. She still wore the devilish little grin. "Not...so...weak," she fumbled over the words.

"And what does that mean?" he asked.

She pointed to the ugly pink scars on his shoulder and arm where he'd been shot.

"Yeah well." Brett said. "My pants. Can I have them please?"

In answer she tossed them on another boulder, this one far from the water's edge.

She giggled. A pleased, musical sound he'd never heard from her before, and then with a swaying, satisfied walk she left.

Infuriating woman.

Brett waited until he was sure she'd gone, then he hurried out of the water and dressed as quick as he could.

His hair was still soaking wet by the time he reached the cabin. Mourning Song was there, working on dinner again, and Red Elk sat lounging in a chair on the porch. The Crow looked first at Mourning Song—she was bent over the fire humming a happy tune —then to a red-faced Brett. His eyes swung to Brett's wet hair and clothes.

Then he threw back his head and laughed long and hard.

"What?" Brett said. "Nothing happened."

The Crow only laughed harder. He wiped at the tears running down from both eyes.

"I warned you about her," Red Elk said once he got his laughter under control.

"It's nothing like that," Brett protested. "You said she'd try to kill me."

"She still might. Women are crazy." Red Elk started laughing again.

Brett looked inside the shack at Mourning Song. He couldn't afford to be distracted, not now. Besides, he'd all but promised Lisa Sweeney he'd come courting when all this business with Davis Judd was over.

"My second wife, Standing Woman, was much the same," Red Elk said. "Fiery temper. Sometimes she would throw things at me, and then afterward she would be so sweet. She would forgive me anything, but she never forgot. Not once."

"She's back on the reservation?" Brett asked. For some reason he couldn't imagine Red Elk living in a teepee on some reservation. He couldn't imagine the proud Crow settling down with a family either. He seemed too carefree and unattached.

"No," the man's face clouded over. "She grew sick one winter a very long time ago. Back when our people still roamed free."

"You have no one then?"

Red Elk gave him a hard look. "I have only my people. Though we are not what we once were." He was quiet for a time. Then he went on, louder this time for Mourning Song to hear. "My first wife was stolen by the Cheyenne."

"Stolen? You didn't go get her?"

Red Elk smiled. "Why would I? She was a horrible woman. Couldn't cook. I stole that Cheyenne warrior's horse and called it even. I feel bad for him sometimes. That was a great horse."

Mourning Song came out of the cabin then.

"Come eat," she said.

Brett gave Red Elk a questioning look.

"She learns quickly," the Crow said.

Brett and Red Elk sat down and took their meal. When they were done eating Mourning Song took her own food, Brett was uncomfortable with her watching them as he ate.

Mother never waited on father like that; we all ate together as one family.

As one family. The thought was there before it struck him as odd. Was this his new family? A Crow Medicine man, a cursed Cheyenne Princess?

Mourning Song cleared her throat. The room was quiet. She began speaking and Red Elk translated for Brett's benefit.

"In the days before the true people came, the Great Spirit soared above the land on a Raven's wings. The land was empty though for the Spirit had created Brother Wolf, and in his greed, Brother Wolf had devoured all that roamed upon the grasslands. The Spirit grieved for the land. In his wisdom he took a handful of branches from the aspen. He breathed life into the branches and the first elk were born. The elk were strong with sharp shining hooves and antlers like spears.

But Brother Wolf was wise. He lay behind the trees or hid in the brush beside the sweetest streams and waited for the elk. And when his brothers were killed the elk grew sad and cried out to the Great Spirit. The Great Spirit took pity on the elk and he lifted the mountains up above the plains and he told the trees they may not climb to the highest peaks and so this gave the elk a refuge.

Brother Wolf cried out to the Great Spirit then. 'First you gave the elk hooves to crush and antlers to stab. Now you give them an empty land to live where I cannot catch them. You have denied me my feast. Would you allow me to starve and for the land to be empty save for the elk?'

The Great Spirit answered Brother Wolf. 'Once a year I will bring the elk down into the low places. But in your greed you would destroy them and then have nothing to eat, so this time will not last and they will soon return to the mountains and out of your reach.'

And so winter came to the mountains and as the snow rose and covered the grass the elk moved down into the low country where

Brother Wolf could hunt. True to the Great Spirit's word though the sun returned bright and clear, the snow melted, the grass returned, and the elk went back to the high open places away from Brother Wolf."

Mourning Song stopped talking then and started clearing away the cookpots. The men shuffled outside to watch the coming twilight.

"What was that about?" Brett asked.

"Often after the evening meal, the Chiefs or Medicine will tell stories," Red Elk said.

"Stories?"

"There is wisdom in such. A great deal can be learned from a good story."

Brett thought about what Mourning Song had said. Elk and wolf, two animals locked in age-old conflict. Winter belonged to the wolf, but the elk did not go quietly. It fought with every tool it had, hoof and antler matched against tooth and claw. He'd seen those great proud bull elk feeding up in the peaks. He could imagine them battling wolves along the craggy rocks and high forests, sharp antlers whipping, hooves flashing. But he'd also seen their bones too. He'd seen them lying scattered and sun-bleached.

Such was the way of things, his father once explained. *Everything has its season.*

Red Elk suddenly grew quiet. He gazed out over the twilight horizon. "Someone is coming?"

Brett studied the night and saw nothing. "Where?"

Red Elk stood. He picked up his rifle and checked the chamber. Then he said something in Cheyenne to Mourning Song. She gave him a serious look and took up her own rifle, the one Brett had bought her in Sheridan. "I will be on your left. She will stay in the cabin with her rifle. I do not think they mean you harm. I think they are lost."

Brett retrieved his rifle and waited beneath the shadowed awning. He still hadn't heard or seen anything, but he knew better than to doubt Red Elk. The Crow didn't seem to think this was real trouble.

That would rule out any Judd riders, but Brett couldn't imagine who else would be prowling up here.

He was starting to think Red Elk had finally been mistaken when he heard the clop of a hoofbeat in the distance. There were several small groves of trees around, aspen and pine mainly, and he saw movement in the shadows near one. Stepping out of the trees, two riders came into view. One of them was tall and slim and the other a good bit shorter.

They saw the shack then and started closer until Brett recognized them. The shorter figure raised her arm. "Brett," she said.

"Lisa, Mr. Sweeney, what are you doing up here?"

"Brett, we need your help," Lisa said.

"My help?"

"Davis Judd sent a warning to Youngston. He's threatening to burn us out."

"Why come to me then? I've accomplished nothing."

"You have accomplished a great deal actually. More than most, against all odds, you have fought back and survived," Gideon interrupted.

"I've had help," Brett said. "Both from you and..."

Red Elk stepped from around the cabin and Mourning Song opened the door. Gideon's eyes widened at the sight of the two Indians.

"Easy now, we are all friends here," Brett said.

Slowly, Gideon relaxed. "As you say."

He noticed Lisa giving Mourning Song a hard glare. For her own part, Mourning Song returned the look coolly.

"Gideon won't you come down and tell me what's happened?"

"I'm afraid there's not much to tell," Gideon said. "Lisa already told you most of it, but not why we really came."

He swung down off his horse and came closer. Brett noticed he walked with a limp and hunched over slightly instead of standing tall and straight. When he was closer Brett saw the deep wrinkles beneath his eyes.

It's like he's aged ten years over the last few days.

"And why did you come?"

"We are leaving Brett."

"Because of Davis Judd?"

Gideon nodded. "Him and Kip Lane and others. We have always struggled to survive out here, but now it is worse. You already know what happened to James Tolliver and his family. And with Pryor off limits to us we've had to get our supplies from Billings. Several of our wagons have been attacked and robbed."

"Kip Lane?"

Gideon nodded. "He and his men."

"Where will you go?"

"Home. Back to Salt Lake City."

"Please help us Brett," Lisa interjected.

"Lisa please, that is enough. This isn't his fight and there's little he can do to change an entire territory. I've made up my mind already. We are going home."

"At least tell him everything," Lisa said.

Gideon straightened a little. He looked off into the high mountain peaks as if he were unsure about saying more.

"What else?" Brett asked.

"Kip Lane." Gideon ran a hand up into his hair and tugged at it. "Kip Lane has told everyone in Pryor we won't make it outside of Wyoming. He plans on burning down Youngston and killing all of us."

"I'm sorry Gideon."

"This is not your fault son," Gideon rested a hand on the Brett's shoulder. "I hope you'll come with us. It would mean the world to Lisa."

Brett glanced back at her. Still in the saddle, she gave him a hopeful look.

"I don't know..."

Gideon sighed. "You don't have to decide now. It will take us a few days to pack everything up and, if you change your mind, you are welcome to join us on the trail. Lisa we have to be getting on home."

"Brett please come with us," Lisa begged.

"Lisa, I want to. Really I do, but I don't know..."

"We have to be going," Gideon interrupted. "We have much to prepare for our long journey."

With that, Gideon mounted up and started down the mountain toward Youngston. Lisa stayed at her father's side, but she kept looking back.

When they were almost out of sight, Brett waved. Lisa did not return it.

He looked at the mining shack. Mourning Song was watching him from the lit doorway, eyes dark and serious.

What had passed between her and Lisa?

"They are weak," she said.

"Weak?" Brett answered. "No, they are just worried about their families. They have children to protect."

"Then fight." With that she gave him a disgusted look and went back inside.

"What will you do now?" Red Elk asked.

"I have to end this. Somehow I have to end all of this."

———

THE DAY'S first crimson light found Brett and Red Elk riding for Pryor.

Brett had one thought and one thought only on his mind. He didn't yet know how, but he was going to kill Davis Judd and Kip Lane.

It's the only way to stop this.

Before sunrise, they'd circled around to come into town from the south, few people traveled this way, and were within sight of town when a familiar rider caught Brett's eye. Though he hadn't seen her since that night in the alley, he would have recognized Allie and her little mare anywhere. Sure she hadn't seen them yet, he reigned in.

"We'll follow her," Brett said.

"You know this girl?" Red Elk asked.

"I do," Brett said. He did not explain their shared history to Red

Elk. The pain of Allie's betrayal was still too raw. "She will lead us to Lane."

For two hours they followed her. Allie rode quickly but never beyond a fast trot. She went east toward the mountains then swung a little south before turning east once again into a steep-sided canyon.

Brett paused at the canyon's mouth.

"If we catch her she can lead us to Kip Lane."

"I do not like this place," Red Elk said. He eyed the rocky walls warily. Then he studied the trail below. Brett's eyes followed his.

Allie's tracks were plain enough, but there were older prints as well. Tracks from many horses.

"There could be any number of men in there," Red Elk said. "Maybe this Lane and his friends."

"Good. Then we can end this now." Brett drew his rifle and started Cimarron forward.

The canyon wasn't large, no wider than a quarter-mile at the mouth. There was a clear gravel-bottomed creek winding down out of it, and either bank was covered in thick grass broken up with clumps of scattered brush or trees and the occasional lumpy boulder. In half an hour Brett could see the end of the canyon tapering up toward the mountain. He'd lost sight of Allie though and that troubled him. Her path was plain enough—she made no effort to hide it —due east, turning only to avoid obstacles.

Gradually, Brett noticed a faint roaring in his ears and the wind blowing down from the mountain smelled of fresh rain.

"Do you—" he started to ask.

Red Elk cut him off with a sharp look and a finger held to his mouth. The Crow dismounted and tied his horse to a cedar sapling. Brett followed his lead.

Rifles drawn, they stalked forward. The thorny brush grew thicker here, pressed in tight all around except where the stream cut through it.

Allie had ridden through a narrow passage, barely wider than a horse, and they followed on foot. Brett's shirt snagged a branch and, not wanting to make a sound, he used the tip of his knife to pry the thorns free. He pressed on and the brush thinned until turning into a shaded grove of towering pine and aspen. The roaring sound grew louder as they went and the smell of rain was stronger.

As they neared the edge of a clearing, Red Elk took the lead. He hunched down into a crouch, darting tree-to-tree like a ghost. Brett matched him as best he could.

At the edge of the trees Red Elk knelt behind a clump of tall grass. Brett slid down on his belly to get as low as possible. He climbed forward on elbows and knees until he could see out.

His eye was drawn first to the source of the sound, a ribbon of water cascading down off the mountain and thundering into a blue pool. Mist rolled out from the waterfall's base like a low-hanging cloud. He saw the cabins next. There were three in all, the nearest a little one-room affair with an attached corral, not unlike his own mining shack.

He saw Allie then, riding slowly toward that first cabin. Kip Lane and three more men, none Brett recognized, came out and started toward her. Lane wasn't more than two hundred yards off. Brett had taken shots of that distance and further while out hunting often enough.

Lane will never know what hit him.

He tucked the rifle into his shoulder, aimed down along the barrel. Before he could fire though, sunlight flashed off the front sight, and one of Lane's men cried out.

Lane's pistol appeared like lightning and, despite the distance, he began firing. Brett squeezed off his own shot, and hurried as it was missed completely. Bullets whizzed and crashed into the tree trunks all around. Brett ducked down where he'd be less of a target. At least one of the other men must have held a rifle as he heard the deep booming echo with every shot.

Brett risked a glance. Instead of retreating to the cabin, Lane and his men were advancing. Two now held rifles and Lane was reloading one of his pistols. Worse, there were four more men near the farthest cabins gathering their horses.

We've slapped a hornet's nest. Half the Judd outfit must be down in here.

Beside a pale aspen trunk, Red Elk rose up on one knee. The Crow was the picture of calm as he squeezed off a shot and the nearest rifleman dropped.

The Crow ducked back around the aspen before a half dozen bullets bit into the soft wood.

"Too many. Let's go," Brett yelled.

Showing his white teeth, Red Elk smiled and nodded. He slid another cartridge into the big Sharps. "I agree."

Brett lifted up and cut loose with his rifle. He fired quickly, not bothering to aim, working the lever as fast as he could, emptying the gun in only seconds. To his surprise the second rifleman yelped and fell while Lane and the last man dove into the grass and dropped out of sight. The men at the far cabins still struggled to get their horses under control. The sound of so much gunfire echoing off the granite walls must have driven the animals wild.

Then he and Red Elk were off and running for the gap.

Retrieving their horses, they took to the trail out and noticed a group of four riders advancing up the canyon from below. The new riders saw them at the same time, grabbing for their guns. They were close, well within pistol range, and Brett's Colt sprang to life. He cut the nearest newcomer down with a pair of quick shots. The others broke and scattered for cover.

Too many. There are too many. He and Red Elk were outnumbered and more of Lane's men would be closing in from behind. Moreover the mounted men were still between them and the canyon's entrance.

"Follow me," Red Elk said without hesitating. The Crow swung his pony toward the canyon's near wall. The riders had regrouped now; they had their guns out and were riding up fast. Turning in the saddle, flame blossomed from Brett's Colt as he emptied it and then let Cimarron have his head.

Though missing, his fire sent their pursuers clambering aside and they fell back.

Red Elk found a narrow game trail and bolted up the steep wall.

The Crow's horse scrambled over loose rock along a ledge no more than a yard wide. Brett hesitated at the bottom.

Surely there is another way.

A gunshot ricocheted off the wall and made up his mind. More shots followed as the big stallion raced up the ledge. He heard the boom from a rifle and a shot bounced off the wall directly ahead of him. Then suddenly they were over the top. Red Elk set a quick pace directly away from the canyon.

Brett cursed his luck. *We failed completely and worse...they'll be trailing us now. We've got find a way to lose them.*

14

Leading the way, the Crow brought them up along another trail, this one ancient and worn deep in the stony soil. After a time Brett recognized it.

"This is the trail up to the Medicine Wheel?"

"Yes," Red Elk agreed. He looked back over the distance.

Brett could see a cloud of brown dust rising up far behind. "How many?"

"Six at least to raise so much dust," Red Elk said. "And there are others fanning out to the west."

"They are herding us. Like wolves they are pushing us into a trap somewhere."

"Yes."

But where were they leading them? Brett's mind traced over the land. "If they stay spread out they will discover the cabin. We have to lead them up into the pass or they'll stumble across it."

"They have men waiting in the passes as well," Red Elk said. He pointed his rifle toward the mountain and Brett saw a column of black smoke rising up in sporadic puffs.

"How?" Brett started. He looked back toward the narrow canyon they'd escaped. A second column of black smoke lifted there. He understood then. "Judd must have kept men in the high pass waiting for us to cross over with a second herd to Sheridan. They signaled them with the smoke."

"As you say," Red Elk shrugged.

While they spoke another column rose up from somewhere near Pryor.

"No way to go but north. We've got to reach the mine before they do. We've got to get Mourning Song out." Brett's stomach turned at the thought of Judd's men capturing her again.

Capture? Brett thought about the fierce Cheyenne woman. *No, she'll die before she allows herself to be taken again.*

They pressed north at a fast clip. They couldn't run the horses the whole way; the distance was too great. An hour south of the cabin, riding through a line of thick cedars, they spotted a line of riders moving in from the west to cut them off. Red Elk reigned in.

"We can't slip past. Between the mountains and the open plains they've got us boxed. They are on all sides," Brett said.

"Yes." Red Elk studied the riders ahead. "But these have not seen us yet."

Brett checked his rifle and then his Colt. Both were full. There was a little draw ahead with cottonwoods spread along its shallow banks. "Let's get to that draw. Then we'll open up on them once they make the clearing."

They reached the draw just seconds before the men ahead came into view. There were five in total, spread out a good hundred feet from one another.

"Keep your eyes peeled. They've got to come through here," a tall man near the center said. "We've got 'em on all sides."

The speaker wore a loose red bandana around his neck and Brett drew a bead on it.

He pointed to the man and then swept his hand to the east. Red Elk nodded and sighted in on his own target.

The distance was less than a fifty yards when Brett fired. His first shot took the man dead-center and Brett shifted his aim to the man over on his right. Though surprised, the Judd men got into action quickly. Their guns belched smoke and bullets struck all around. Brett fired twice more then—without pausing to see if he'd hit—adjusted further down the line. A bullet kicked up a handful of dirt in front of him. He snapped a quick shot at the man on the farthest east then swung back. One of the riders was almost on top of him. The man fired and a Brett felt the wind from the bullet pass near his face. Brett's own shot sent the man running.

Then as suddenly as it started the shooting was over.

"How many did we miss?" Brett asked.

"Two slipped away to the west," the Indian held his rifle awkwardly.

"Two to tell the others where we are," Brett scowled. "And you? Are you alright?"

"I will live. Only a lucky shot." The Crow turned where Brett could see an ugly wound near his elbow. "Get the horses while I bind this."

Soon enough Brett and the injured warrior were on their way north again. This time they pushed their horses hard. No doubt Judd's other hunting parties had heard the shots. Brett could almost feel them closing in now that their quarry had revealed itself.

Brett leapt out of the saddle in front of the shack. He burst through the door to find Mourning Song tanning a deerhide. He took a breath he hadn't realized he'd even been holding.

She is alright. Now I've only got to keep her safe.

"Pack your things. We've got to go."

She nodded, understanding enough of what he'd said, and quickly began to gather her belongings. Brett went back outside to get her Palomino ready. Still in the saddle, Red Elk met him. The Crow swayed a little and blood had soaked through the bandage. He looked very pale.

"Do you need help down?" Brett said. "I can get you one of the other horses. A fresh one."

For a long time Red Elk stared out over the long distance to the south. Finally, he turned back to Brett with a little grin. "Will you drive some of your cattle to my people?"

"I will after we survive." Brett shook his head. "We've no time for this now though. We need to be gone when they arrive."

Brett moved to the corral and started saddling Mourning Song's palomino. They'd bring all the horses. He'd keep Cimarron of course. Though the stallion had run hard already, he would still outpace the others.

"There is never enough time, but we only have what we are given," Red Elk said. "I thank you, little brother. You have given me life these last months. You have given me everything the Spirits promised and more."

"And that is?"

Red Elk hoisted his rifle. "A good death."

"What?"

The Crow turned his horse to face south back over their trail. "Ride hard my friend. I will see you again one day."

"Red Elk please don't—"

The Crow let out a war cry and slapped his heels against his horse's flanks. Then they were gone, racing south in a rising column of dust.

Brett watched after him.

The proud warrior paused on a hill less than a half-mile to the south. Red Elk spun his horse in a circle. He raised the big Sharps overhead in a wave. Then he took aim at something unseen further south. Smoke rolled from the barrel, and Red Elk raised the gun triumphantly. Reloading quickly, he ran his horse east up the mountain.

Brett knew the area well, where Red Elk rode the grassy hillside lay open for some distance and then met the granite walls of the Bighorns as they rose up in sheer cliffs. There was no hope of escape.

Mourning Song came out to stand beside Brett. She followed his gaze to the south. "Go?" she said.

"Yes." Brett turned to her. There were tears on her cheeks. "We have to go now."

He helped her onto her Palomino and they led the other horses northward. Behind them he heard the occasional boom of the Sharps interrupted by many cracks of smaller rifles.

Then all was silent.

———

BRETT AND MOURNING Song slowly swung around from due north to west. They passed a mile north of Youngston, and Brett paused on a windswept ridge to look down over the Mormon settlement. The village was a beehive of activity. Men and women were arranging furniture into white-canvassed wagons waiting outside their homes. The older children were either helping, watching younger siblings, or gathering the livestock into pens and barns.

Gideon has them hustling to load up.

If Brett had any doubts about the Mormon's conviction to leave they were gone now. *It isn't too late to go west with them.*

He could easily swing down there into town and be welcome. They'd welcome Mourning Song too of course, though he still didn't know what it was that had passed between her and Lisa back at the cabin.

But if I go down this road I'll never get the ranch back. Someday I might have children of my own and what will I tell them if I cut and run now? That I left when things got hard. That I let their inheritance slip away because I was afraid.

Beyond the overlook, further west, he and Mourning Song dropped down into the empty badlands. There were hundreds of small canyons here, all branching off like a thousand tiny roots feeding into the Shoshone. At random Brett dropped down off the sage-covered flats into one, and for a time they held to its winding path snaking lower into bigger and bigger canyons. Brett found a trickle of water running out of one branch and turned off toward the source of the little stream. A half hour later, at a sharp bend, they found a clearing with about an acre of grass and set their camp.

Somewhere during all the fighting, Brett had picked up a bullet burn along his ribs. He didn't notice it until they were camped.

Without a word, Mourning Song helped him strip out of his shirt and began caring for the wound.

Brett couldn't help but stare at her as she worked. He was struck then by how much he admired her. She was a fighter for sure. She'd been placed into the worst situation imaginable, her own people regarded her as cursed, and then she'd been taken by Judd's men to be sold for profit in Deadwood. Against all odds she'd been freed by a pair of sworn enemies in Red Elk and himself. In the end though—unlike the other women they'd freed—her people hadn't wanted her back.

And so now she's here with me even after Red Elk sacrificed himself to save us. But why stay? He didn't believe she was here purely to repay a debt. *Does she truly have nowhere else to be?*

Mourning Song laid out the meal as usual then knelt by the fire and waited for him to eat.

Brett had never been comfortable with the arrangement. With Red Elk he'd decided to tolerate it, but now Mourning Song's attention focused exclusively at him.

"Please," he gestured across from himself. "Please sit and eat with me."

Mourning Song tilted her head to one side.

"Please."

She took Red Elk's customary place. Brett picked up the piece of thick leather and offered it to her.

"Go on. Take some." He had no idea how much she understood, but he suspected she caught most of it.

Tentative at first, with an almost-frightened look, she took a small helping of meat. She ate slowly. She looked down at her food or hands mostly, but occasionally she snuck a glance at him.

She seems almost...what? Meek? Not a word he would he would have ever used to describe her.

"It is good. Thank you," he said when he caught her eye.

"Welcome," she said.

Brett waited for her to grow angry like she had before when he'd thanked her, but this time she seemed to accept his praise.

She reached for one of the tin cups and Brett caught up the water-skin. She seemed embarrassed and fidgeted with her fingers while he poured.

"Thank...you," she said.

"Welcome," he said with a little smile.

Gradually, the tension left her shoulders and she seemed to relax. She looked out into the deepening night and then up at the sky. There was a new moon tonight and the stars shone bright and clear. A family of coyotes howled out in the distance.

Brett fell into his old habit of drawing his Colt over and over. Seth Nelson, the gunfighter living in his cabin, had been right. Filing the front sight smooth made a huge difference.

Enough to match Kip Lane?

He doubted it. He thought about what else Nelson had said. Accuracy, aiming true, making the first shot count, these mattered more than pure speed. While he practiced his thoughts drifted.

Red Elk, his best and only real ally, was surely dead. At least a dozen men had taken out after him. The old warrior was wily for sure. He wouldn't go down easy, but no one could escape so many.

Gideon Sweeney and the people of Youngston were leaving. They hadn't done much—or anything really—in the way of fighting, but they had nursed him back to health and sold him supplies occasionally. And it had been a comfort to have a safe haven among them. He'd enjoyed talking with Lisa. She was a great listener and he felt... lighter after spending time with her.

Mourning Song rose and started to put away their things.

The Cheyenne woman was strong, no doubt about that. She'd stuck with him through all of this out of some misguided sense of honor. Now that Red Elk was gone she was his only companion, and he wasn't sure if she understood anything he said.

Myself and one Cheyenne woman I can't speak to against Davis Judd, two gunfighters, and all his other hired men.

It wasn't much. Brett drew the Colt again. It felt good in his hand. Solid.

Against these odds no one expects me to keep fighting. No man would ever have the right to hold it against me. Does it matter though? Outnumbered or not, I have to finish this.

The only way to do that was to face Davis Judd and his gunfighters. He needed to be smart about it. Smarter than he had been. He had to catch them separately. Somehow he had to break Judd and chase him out of the country. He'd tried fighting indirectly, going after the man's cattle, trying to ruin his businesses, burning down his house even. Nothing worked. He needed to fight smarter and—when called for—he needed to fight direct.

Even though he was in the right, the law wouldn't help him. Neither would the politicians. The Governor was friends with the Cattleman's Association. The people of Pryor wouldn't help. They knew what had been done to him. They had plenty of chances and none had risen up to denounce Judd.

No, it's up to me. There is no one else.

Staring into the dying fire, Brett's thoughts turned to the past. Every spring after the long bitter cold of winter the barn needed to be mucked out and, for the last few years, this task fell to him. Brett hated it. The work was backbreaking hard and the air in the barn would be dusty and choking. He'd slip and fall and come up covered in muck. For weeks afterward the smell seemed to linger on everything he touched. The first time he'd done it his father had handed him a pitchfork and shovel and said, "The best way to do an unpleasant task is to just dig in and get it done." His father had been right. No matter how much he hated cleaning out the barn or how much he delayed it still had to be done.

Brett spun the cylinder on his Colt. *Tomorrow I start mucking Davis Judd out of Wyoming.*

15

With his rifle ready, Brett lay behind a fallen log on the slope overlooking the trail from Sheridan to Pryor. The day was young, overcast, with low rolling clouds, the dull sky a slate-gray. He'd sworn he wasn't going to fight Davis Judd indirectly anymore, but he couldn't allow the gold from Deadwood to arrive. If Judd got his hands on that he could hire a dozen gunfighters.

Besides, more than anything he needed a way to separate Judd from his two hired gunmen; Brett had an idea on how. First though he had to stop that gold.

Soon enough he heard the creak and rattle of a wagon rumbling up the rocky trail. Brett lifted himself up on one elbow to peer out over the log.

Three men guarded the gold, two riding in the wagon, a double-barreled shotgun propped up on the wooden seat between them. Mounted on a buckskin dun, the third man rode his horse slightly ahead. He paused occasionally considering the hillside, the open drop off to the south, the trail ahead.

Brett wasn't worried about being spotted. Other than his head and part of his shoulders the log hid the rest of him and his clothing matched the ground behind almost perfectly.

He sighted in on the driver. The outrider would be the most dangerous, but if he killed the driver first it would also keep the second rider out of the fight as he struggled to control the team.

He felt a pang at attacking these men from ambush, but Davis Judd and his thugs had forced him into this. He shoved the feeling aside. He couldn't allow doubt to creep in. *Certainly Judd didn't feel any when he sent all those men out to kill me, and Kip Lane hadn't felt any when he backshot me and left me to die alone in the dark.*

They've hunted me like a wild animal and now I have become one.

His bullet took the driver though the chest. The man dropped the reins just as Brett had hoped. He shifted his aim to the outrider and snapped off two quick shots. Both missed. Quickly, the outrider spurred his horse into a run, bobbing and weaving through the screen of trees below.

The man started firing back. Bullets clipped the log and sent leaves flying all around.

Brett took a deep breath. He did his best to ignore the bullets. He sighted along the barrel and squeezed off another round. This one knocked the rider from the saddle and sent him rolling back downhill.

He stood and started for the wagon. The last man was just getting control of the team when Brett stepped out onto the trail. He held his rifle at waist level.

The driver gave him a measuring look. He had the reins in his hands, but Brett saw the shotgun's stock still lying on the seat beside him.

"Don't," Brett said. "Tie off the team and step down and I won't harm you."

The last man looked at the body beside him and then the outrider sprawled face up on the hill. "I'm not sure I believe you."

"If I wanted to kill you I would have done it already."

"You do that and I'll drop these reins and these horses will scatter whatever you're after from here to hell and back."

"You don't know what's in the wagon?"

"Supplies and freight," the man said.

"You don't know about the forty thousand in gold dust then?"

"No." He licked his lips. His eyes darted to the shotgun then back to Brett. "I know I've got a scattergun handy though."

"And I've got this rifle." Brett swung the barrel a few inches. "Think you can reach the gun before I blow you off that wagon."

"Like I said. You do that," the driver licked his lips, "and these horses will go crazy. You'll have hell catchin them. If they don't go over the side and dump that gold. Sides, I might get lead into you. Scattergun's a terrible thing at this range. Don't even have to aim."

"You work for Judd?"

"Signed on two weeks ago."

"You know who I am then?"

"I do." The man nodded.

"No doubt Judd's told you I burned down his house and killed quite a few of his men. You just saw what I did to your two partners here."

"Barely knew em before this trip."

"If you're inclined to live and let live, maybe we can come to some sort of arrangement."

For a long moment the last man said nothing. Brett felt the tension gather. He was going to have to kill this man.

"Well, what do you have in mind?"

The wagon was loaded heavy with flour and sugar and salt, but beneath the other freight, cleverly hidden under the floorboards of the wagon were four bags, each filled with Black Hills gold dust. The driver took one—he wasn't greedy he claimed—and headed back over the pass as fast as his team would carry him.

Brett loaded up his packhorse with the other three and set a quick pace for the mining shack.

He circled the mine twice, looking for tracks or other sign, and to his surprise it still didn't look like Judd's men had found the place.

Likely they forgot to look after Red Elk led them away into the peaks. One more debt I owe you, my friend.

Brett put one of the sacks in the old mineshaft, and covered it with loose debris. He looked around the little cabin. Though small and leaky and cold the old cabin had been his home for a long time now. Without Red Elk and Mourning Song—he'd left her back at their camp west of Youngston—the place seemed painfully empty. Then he set out for Youngston with the other two bags.

Gideon Sweeney met him with a big smile as he rode in.

"You've decided to join us," he said. "Lisa will be pleased. We're setting out day after tomorrow bright and early."

"I'm not going with you," Brett said. He dropped down and unloaded one of the heavy bags on the back of Sweeney's wagon. "I brought you some traveling money though."

Gideon studied the bag. "What is this?"

"Gold dust," Brett said.

"Where did you get it?"

"Doesn't matter. What matters is I'm giving it to you. There should be enough there to help your family and even these others start a new life again."

"Brett I can't possibly accept this. You stole it didn't you?"

"Like I said. Don't worry about where it came from. Davis Judd owed me for my trouble. It's mine and now I've given it to you."

It isn't strictly a lie; Judd has been grazing on the ranch and had one of his men living in my cabin for almost a year now. I deserve some sort of compensation. Brett smiled to himself. The rate might be a little steep, but Judd never negotiated that properly now did he.

"I cannot accept this," Gideon shook his head. The disapproval on his face was plain.

Jane Sweeney stepped up beside her husband. "Yes Gideon, you can. We need this and you know it. We've lost everything leaving this place."

Gideon gave her a long look. "As you say wife," he finally agreed. Then he turned to Brett again. "I can never repay you."

"Think of it as me buying you all out."

Gideon lifted a hand toward the village. "This place, our land, it isn't worth so much."

"It is to me," Brett said.

Gideon patted the bag. "I would rather have you with us than this."

"I can't leave here. Not yet and maybe not ever. I've got to see this through."

"Even if it kills you? Your father and mother wouldn't want that," Jane said.

"Even so," Brett said with a rueful half-smile.

"Will you at least say goodbye to Lisa?" Gideon asked.

"Yes. I owe her that."

"She's in the barn feeding the team," Jane said.

At the barn door Brett paused. He could see inside, where Lisa was busy scooping corn by the handful into each horse's bin. He stopped for a time just watching her. He noticed how the sunbeams streamed in from the open windows and lit her silken hair. Her long blue dress shifted as she moved. She was certainly beautiful, moreso than Allie had ever been. What had he seen in her? It seemed a different life before Allie betrayed him.

Lisa finished with the last horse, turned toward the door, and froze when she saw him.

Time stretched for a moment. Brett imagined he would remember this instant—the smell of the corn and the dust and the hay, the sound of the horses eating, the way Lisa stood, the way she looked at him, eyes alive and hopeful and cautious all at once—for the rest of his life.

She spoke then. "You aren't going with us."

"No."

"Why not?"

"I can't give up my ranch."

"It's just a place. There are lots of places. You can come with us and find a new ranch, a better ranch. Please Brett. I know we could be so happy."

"I can't run from this. I have to end it."

"Is it because of her?"

"Who?" Brett asked. He didn't understand what she meant.

"You know who Brett." Lisa's face reddened. For a split second her eyes flared.

"No...I don't," he said. Her tone had shifted. He didn't recognize it at first. She sounded angry. He'd never heard her this way before. *She is upset, and not just because I won't go with them. Then why?*

"That Indian girl."

Brett wasn't sure who she meant for a time. Then he shook his head. There could only be one Indian girl. "Mourning Song. No, it isn't because of her."

"I don't believe you," Lisa's eyes narrowed a little.

"Lisa, I swear this isn't about her. This is about me and Davis Judd."

"But why?"

"Because I have to take back what's mine."

For a long time, neither spoke.

"Your father is right Lisa. Wyoming is a tough land, but I have to end this for my own sake. I can't run anymore. I've tried beating Judd a dozen different ways, but he understands only strength. I've got to face him or I'll never be able to face myself."

"Then will you come afterward? When all of this is over will you come west with us? To me?" Lisa pleaded. Her voice broke and tears welled up in her eyes.

"I will."

This was it then. He had to face down Judd and Kip Lane, and when it was over he'd ride after the Sweeneys and join them. He and Lisa could be together. He still had two more bags of gold dust and a good bit of money leftover from Curly Red's reward and robbing Judd's house. Selling the ranch would only add to his wealth. He could ride up to the cabin and get his mother's ring and then catch up to Lisa. He would ask Gideon's blessing and they could be together.

"Nothing would make me happier," Brett said.

———

LEAVING YOUNGSTON, Brett rode hard for his parent's cabin. The morning clouds had burned away and the sun hung just past midday, shining down hot and sullen. The air was deathly still. On stifling days like this he missed the feel of a cold breeze on his face.

He slowed Cimarron when he drew close to the cabin, and he left the big stallion in the same grove of spruce he'd hidden in after climbing out of that dank crevasse. Brett flexed the fingers of his right hand; he felt good. Alive. How far he'd come since that black day?

Pistol in his left hand and a bag of gold tucked beneath his other arm, he crept to the cabin. Quietly, he came around the barn just as before. The corrals were empty. Seth Nelson wasn't there just as he'd hoped. He needed to avoid the wily gunfighter. His plan was to frame Nelson for stealing Judd's gold, and then provoke a fight between him and either Judd or Lane.

Let them fight each other, he reasoned. At the very least he'd only have two enemies to face then. *And with a bit of luck there might only be one.*

Brett took a breath and started out across the hard-packed ground between the barn and cabin. He stopped on the porch to risk a glance in one of the curtained windows. No sign of Nelson. He checked a second window; this time his mother's curtains blocked his view. He'd have to chance it.

Colt leading the way, he stepped inside.

Seth Nelson sat at the dining table, one hand covering his stomach, the other clutching a pistol pointed at Brett.

"Come back to offer me that job I see? I'd happily accept, but I'm afraid you're a little late," Nelson said. He winced as he said it and Brett noticed blood dribbling down from his chair into a puddle on the floor.

"Looks like it," Brett said. "Lane?"

Nelson smiled a little and nodded. He looked at Brett's Colt. "Shall we shoot it out?"

"I'd rather not. I was hoping you'd kill Lane for me."

"Kip's gone crazy. Either you or the Indian shot off most of his right ear. Marked him good. Burned his scalp with a nasty scar too. Kip's always been vain."

"I must have winged him when we ran out of the canyon."

"You knocked him cold. Bullet didn't go through his skull though just sliced him up some." Nelson eyed the gold tucked under Brett's arm. "That from Judd's wagon?"

"It is."

Nelson smiled. "Well, at least you brought money this time."

"I'd planned on framing you for holding up the wagon. Then I figured I'd step back to let you and Judd and Lane shoot it out."

"Not a bad plan, but your timing was off. Kip already made his move."

"Over this?" Brett lifted the bag.

"No, he's been aching for a go at me for years. And like I said, since you scarred him up, he's gone loco. Gut shot me yesterday evening as I was sitting out on the porch."

"Long before I hit the wagon," Brett nodded. "Any idea where he is now?"

"Feeling bold?" Nelson grinned again. "Lane's good. He is very, very good. Fast and accurate both." He paused a moment. "Mind if I lower my gun?"

"Go ahead," Brett said.

"Glad to see you took my advice and filed that front sight off," Nelson shrugged. He set the gun aside. "Other than you stealing back your horse I've no real reason to shoot you. Mine's empty anyway. I was half-hoping you'd put me out of my misery. It hurts like hell."

The gunman smiled, but Brett could see the pain in his eyes. There was a quake to his voice.

"Figured out who I am then." Brett holstered his gun. He set the gold on a chair near the door. "Cimarron gave it away?"

"That is a fine horse. I took care of your pa's cabin best I could. Never was much of a homebody."

"Thanks for that. I saw you replaced the third step on the porch. The board cracked and broke the winter before Pa killed himself."

"Killed himself?" Seth said with a little snort. "Your pa didn't kill himself."

"What?" The room was deathly silent.

"Me and Davis and Kip met your pa on the road to Pryor. We were on our way out here to buy him out. Only your pa didn't like the offer. Took it as an insult. Judd didn't hold to that so we hung your pa beneath the big old cottonwood on the road to Pryor. You know the one where your ranch meets the trail to Youngston."

Brett's pulse thundered. His breath shallowed. He wasn't hot inside...no...he was cold, cold like winter ice on the highest peak.

Nelson went on. "Davis figured you'd sell easy enough and Kip sent that devil girl of his out to talk you into it. We didn't want to kill you. Too many people dying all at once might draw attention we didn't want." Nelson paused and swallowed. "Kip though, he got worried his girl was getting sweet on you. He thought she might talk you into the deal and then both of you would up and vanish. And Kip well, he can't stand to lose."

Brett couldn't believe what he was hearing. *My father didn't kill himself. Davis Judd and his men murdered him for the ranch.*

And this man sitting in front of me helped.

The Colt was in his hand before he'd even thought about drawing. Twice it barked and Nelson jerked with each bullet. In the confines of the cabin, the sound was impossibly loud. There were two black holes, perfectly round and almost touching, in the center of the gunman's chest. Smoke curled up from the end of the Colt's barrel in a little gray tendril.

"Not bad," Nelson wheezed. "You might even be a match for Kip. He'll be out hitting Youngston tonight. Watch Davis though he—"

Whatever else Seth Nelson meant to say died on his lips.

For a long time Brett didn't move. Davis Judd and Kip Lane killed his father. Had it been a trick? Maybe Nelson lied so Brett would end his suffering.

No, that doesn't make sense. It has to be more than that. If he'd only wanted me to kill him he could have threatened me with the pistol. Brett certainly hadn't thought it was empty when he came in. Besides how would Nelson have known about the cottonwood tree? Few enough people knew his father took his own life, only Bill Hollis for sure; Brett never told anyone exactly where he'd found his body.

He wanted to make sure I'd go after Lane and Judd. He's set me up to take his revenge for him.

It was then that Nelson's final words struck him like a hammer. *He'll be out hitting Youngston tonight.*

16

Cimarron thundered over the trail, mane flying, hooves thumping like rumbling drums. Brett leaned down over the horse's heaving neck and held on for dear life. The big stallion seemed to know his urgency and needed little encouragement. He had to reach Youngston; he had to warn Gideon and the Mormons that they were out of time. Kip Lane was coming today.

Two miles out Brett saw smoke, black and billowing, rising into the blue Wyoming sky like blood gushing from an open wound.

Too late. I'm too late to stop it.

How many lives were now lost to Kip Lane and his thugs? The Tollivers, Doctor Wahlquist, the Sweeney's, Lisa even? Gone because he hadn't ridden fast enough to warn them.

There might be survivors though. Brett would do what he could to help them and then...and then he would ride out after Kip Lane.

Grudgingly, he slowed Cimarron to a walk. Even the great stallion had his limits, and he wasn't about to kill his horse in a now-futile quest. By the time he reached the edge of Youngston the dying western sun bathed the land in orange and crimson. To Brett's eye it seemed the whole world was covered in blood.

Smoke and flames still rose from at least four houses and most of the barns. Somewhere a horse screamed in pain; there was a shot and then merciful silence. There were several horses and oxen lying dead, many secure in their harnesses. Families stood at their wagons, watching the glowing embers, holding each other tight. Some were not so lucky.

There were several men dead, their wives hunched over their bodies and crying while bewildered children looked on.

He passed a weeping man sitting alone on a stump as he held a dead child. His wife was nowhere to be seen.

A few of the Mormons saw him ride in. Their faces bore streaks of gray ash mixed with tears. The children recoiled in fear. *They can't understand why men came and burned down their homes.* Their parents were angry, understandably so. They gave him hard glares and clenched fists.

Brett faced them. He wanted that pain and anger burned into his memory when he faced Kip Lane. He had caused this. These people had been his friends when he had none, and with Davis Judd's blessing Kip Lane punished them for it.

I can never make this right. But I can take vengeance for what they've done here.

Gideon Sweeney stood looking at a pile of glowing ashes that only this morning had been their barn. Their formerly white-painted house was covered in a layer of ash and grime. Torches scored black marks where they'd been pitched up against its walls.

Each of Gideon's boys held rifles. The girls, excepting Lisa, were comforting their mother. Lisa alone stood with her father.

Gideon turned to regard Brett; he didn't speak.

"Gideon, I am..." Brett started.

"This isn't your fault," Gideon interrupted. "They would have come regardless."

"No. They came because you were a friend to me. They know that. That's why they came." Brett tossed down the bag of gold he'd been planning on framing Seth Nelson with. "Take that along with what I left earlier and start out again. I will catch up to you."

"We will be leaving late tomorrow. Before we go we have to

prepare—" Gideon's voice cracked. He turned his eyes to the nearest smoldering house where the Tollivers had lived. "We have to prepare our friends for the journey home. I won't leave them to be buried here in this cruel place."

"You are going to face them?" Lisa said.

"I am," Brett nodded. "For this and...Seth Nelson told me they murdered my father."

"I thought he was lost in a blizzard," Lisa said.

"I told people that, but the truth is I found him hanging from the big cottonwood tree on the trail to Pryor. I didn't want people to think less of him."

"And now this Nelson claims they murdered him?" Gideon said. "You believe him?"

"They did it because pa wouldn't sell out the ranch to Judd. Nelson knew details I never told anyone."

"You killed him?" Lisa said. A sadness hung in her eyes and it broke Brett to see it.

She looks at me now and sees a killer. Just like the butchers who did this to her friends.

"Kip Lane killed him before I got there. I only helped him out of his misery."

Brett slowly turned toward Pryor. Suddenly he needed to be away from here. He couldn't look at the wreckage of this place or these broken people anymore. He tapped Cimarron's flanks and the stallion picked up speed.

Gideon yelled behind him. "This wasn't your fault Brett. Kip Lane hates us. He would have done it regardless. He was-"

Whatever else Gideon said was lost in the quick beat of Cimarron's hooves. The men who did this wouldn't go far, and Brett knew where they might stop for the night. A place just down the road where they could watch the flames. They would be celebrating no doubt; they wouldn't expect retaliation from Youngston.

They were wrong.

———

A MILE off Brett saw the light from their campfire. It blazed high and bright as if the men gathered around it hadn't a care in the world.

Just as he'd expected, Lane's men had made their camp on a sandy knoll just a couple miles south of Youngston. There were scattered trees along the approach, but the top was bare and commanded a sweeping view of the country all around.

He rode closer and heard them laughing and snapping off the occasional shot.

What manner of men were these? What kind of men would burn innocent people out of their homes and then celebrate?

Not men at all. Just a pack of wolves. Wolves that need to be put down.

A hundred yards short of their camp, Brett held Cimarron up.

He drew his Colt and checked the shells. He did the same with the second pistol tucked into his belt. Then he replaced both.

He hitched Cimarron up to a short pine, drew the rifle from its scabbard, and crept forward.

There were seven men all scattered around the fire. His eyes roamed over them. Some he recognized, but most were new to him, and Kip Lane was not among them. Brett wasn't sure if he should be angry about that or not. He wanted Lane most of all, but fighting against a smaller group—one that did not include a true gunfighter would be better.

When the day came he had to face Lane he couldn't afford distractions. He didn't plan on giving Lane an even break. Three-to-one, they'd gone against his father. Neither Kip Lane nor Davis Judd would get any allowances from him.

One of the men stood by the fire with a pair of empty whiskey bottles. He tossed the first high overhead while the others all tried shooting it. The bottle crashed unharmed and they hooted and laughed all the louder. Several held their guns in one hand and partially-full bottles in the other.

The man by the fire bent down to scoop up the bottle, and one of his friends fired and dirt flew just a few inches from his hand.

"Dammit Jed, you almost took my fingers off," the bottle thrower yelped.

"I was aiming for it," the shooter slurred.

The others laughed. Then another one said. "Send up another one, Buck. We'll get it this time. Won't we boys?"

The rest whooped their agreement.

The man by the fire, Buck, snatched up the bottle before anyone else could shoot at him. He heaved it up and guns crashed. This time the bottle shattered and spilled the last few drops of whiskey into the fire. The flames flared bright and hot and laughter roared as Buck leaped clear and fell flat on his back.

"Just a little fire Buck. No need to mess yourself. Send up the last bottle, we got er figured now."

"Damn you all," Buck said. "One of you throw the next one."

"No, no come on. Give us one more."

Buck stood then and made a show of dusting off his pants and shirt. He took the second bottle by the neck. He swung up with it and it sailed up overhead, catching the firelight, spinning end over end.

When the bottle was at its peak the men fired, and that's when Brett shot Buck through the eye.

Brett cycled the rifle and—in less than a minute's time—emptied it into the sitting crowd. He drew both pistols. Flame belched from either hand in bright, orange flashes. Drunk as they were the Judd men proved slow to respond but finally they began shooting back. Bullets ricocheted wildly though the trees. Brett kept firing. There wasn't time for accuracy. If he saw movement or the muzzle flash from a gun he snapped off a shot at it. Finally, when both guns were empty he holstered one and knelt behind the trunk of a thick lightning-struck pine to reload. There were moans and cries from the camp, but no more gunfire. If there were any men still upright and able to fight, they were holding their fire waiting for him to give himself away.

Deciding he'd pushed his luck far enough, Brett made his way back to Cimarron. His right side hurt. It felt wet and sticky. He needed to be well away from here before they grew bolder. He couldn't afford to let them hunt after him again; he wanted to get Lane and Judd now, before they knew he was coming.

He rode west for camp and Mourning Song. He needed to rest and get his wound bandaged before he faced Lane.

The moon was just shy of full and the sky was clear enough that he could see. Cimarron wove his way through shadowed cedars and clumps of silver-gray sage. They emerged out onto the empty flats and Brett urged the horse a little faster. He had to be careful; there were prairie dog holes scattered about and Cimarron could easily break a leg. The big horse's vision was good though and Brett trusted him to find a safe path.

More and more Brett had come to appreciate Cimarron. The red stallion had nearly-endless endurance and blistering speed when called upon. After the ranch itself Cimarron might be the best thing his father left behind.

He was surprised his side didn't ache. Other than the wet trickling of blood, he could scarce believe he'd been shot.

Probably just a small wound. Mourning Song can clean it up and I'll be fine.

Between crossing the flats and then weaving through the broken canyon country, it took two hours to reach camp. Twice, he'd taken the wrong turn in the maze of twists and turns and been forced to backtrack. Mourning Song had kept the fire small, unless someone stumbled into their particular branch, and then all the way up to the clearing they would never find it. Except for the fire and a few scattered supplies the camp was deserted when he arrived. Mourning Song was nowhere to be found.

Brett suddenly felt terribly weak.

"Mourning Song," he called.

Where has she gone? Maybe she had decided her debt was paid and it was time to go back to her people. Without her the camp seemed painfully quiet and, just like at the old mine, he felt a heavy sense of loss. Again, he was all alone.

Some men said they were stronger alone, but that didn't match his experience. His father certainly hadn't been stronger after his mother passed and, with Mourning Song and Red Elk both gone he didn't feel stronger, only diminished by their absence.

He climbed down out of the saddle. A short bolt of pain came from his side with the movement and he tried to ignore it.

Must be worse than I thought.

Mourning Song had left him some food along with the little fire, but where the wound was he couldn't reach around to stitch himself up. He'd have to return to Youngston once more and see if their doctor could patch him up enough to fight.

Damned woman. She would leave me at the worst time.

There was a rock beside the fire, one big enough to sit on. Brett took two steps for it and suddenly the pain he'd felt before roared up white-hot and sharp. His hand went to his side and he hunched over to his right. He started to sit then froze. One of the shadows at the edge of the firelight moved away from the trees.

How had Lane's men found the camp? Where did they take Mourning Song? There hadn't been any shots. He was sure she would never let herself be taken again. *I have to find her. I have to save her.*

He wouldn't go down without a fight. Brett's hand started down and then he heard the distinct click of a rifle. They had him dead to rights. But the bullet did not come.

"Fool," Mourning Song said as she came rushing out of the darkness. She threw the rifle down and was suddenly at his side, running her hands all over him. She touched his wound and drew back with an angry hiss.

Before he could protest, she started tearing off his shirt. She spoke to him, but in Cheyenne. He understood none of it. She gave him an angry look.

"What?" he said. "You know I can't understand you."

She ignored him. She moved quickly, first stoking up the fire with a couple of small logs and then putting on a pot of water. Then she began rummaging through her things.

Brett eased down to sit on the rock. He turned so the light shined on his injured side, but couldn't see anything himself. There was a bowl of warm stew and he picked it up and started eating. The stew was hot and he wasn't sure if she'd put beef or lamb in it—maybe something she'd killed herself—but it tasted good.

Mourning Song returned. She threw a needle and thread into the warming water. For the first time since he'd returned he got a good look at her. Her eyes were a puffy and bloodshot.

She's been crying. Probably misses Red Elk more than I do. At least the Crow could speak her language.

The water was soon boiling and she fished out the needle and thread with the tip of her knife. Keeping out of the firelight so she could see, she knelt down beside Brett.

"Is the bullet still in there?" Brett asked. He'd felt around the wound but to him everything just seemed numb.

"No," she said and smacked his hand.

Brett took a shell from his belt loop. First he tapped the lead. Then he put it against the wound. "Is the bullet still in there? You have to take it out."

For a minute she seemed confused. Then Mourning Song looked from the bullet to the wound and nodded. She started to feel around. When he winced she gave him an apologetic look.

"No," she finally said. "Empty."

Empty. The bullet went all the way through then.

"Well I'll leave you to it then."

Mourning Song put the needle in her teeth. She pushed him a little toward the left, took the needle between her fingers, and began to sew.

Brett gritted his teeth through the pain. Once she'd finished stitching him up, she tore some cloth into strips and bandaged the wound. Brett recognized the material. It was the blue and flowered print he'd bought her in Sheridan.

"You didn't have to use that. I wanted you to have it...for a dress or a shirt or something."

Mourning Song only gave him a little smile and shook her head. She wrapped the cloth around his stomach and tightened it.

When she was done she stopped to look at him. This wasn't one of her hard glares; she only seemed worried about him.

"Don't worry," Brett said. "I'll be alright. Besides if I die you can go home."

"Home?" she said.

"Sure, home to your people." Brett nodded and pointed to the south.

Mourning Song shook her head.

"Home." She took his hand and turned it so he was pointing back toward the east.

Toward the ranch.

She looked deep in his eyes and slowly ran a hand over his cheek. Her lips were parted and her breathing was quick.

Brett felt his chest growing hot. Gentle as it was, her touch caught his blood to flame. A hunger burned in Brett that he did not recognize.

She smiled then—bigger this time. Brighter than he'd ever seen. She seemed pleased with herself. Then, she stood and moved off to her blankets humming to herself.

Brett watched her go. The heat from her touch faded.

What a strange woman. From the first instant he'd seen her back in that cage she'd hated him. Now, just a short time later, she'd become almost tender. *Natural enough I guess, with Red Elk gone she has no one else left.*

Brett drew his Colt and pointed it into the night. His right side might be hurting but drawing with his left felt smooth and quick as ever. Tomorrow he would need that. Tomorrow he would end this fight and avenge his father.

17

The rising sun hung low when Brett reigned in, still touching the gray Bighorns as if reluctant to begin the new day. He and Mourning Song were on a grassy windswept hillside overlooking Pryor. Mourning Song—looking serene and confident—brought her Palomino up beside Cimarron. She sat tall in the saddle, queenly, and studied the sleepy town like it was an enemy castle to be conquered and brought into her kingdom.

Brett's side hurt, but it wasn't crippling. For the second time that morning, he checked his rifle and then the two pistols.

One way or another, today is the day my business with Davis Judd will finally be over.

Looking back over these last months he realized what a fool he'd been. Over half a year had passed since he'd been shot. He'd tried being indirect, stealing back his cattle, hoping for the law or the politicians to intervene, even going so far as to burn down Judd's house. Foolish all of it.

I would have been better off riding into Pryor and gunning Judd down in the street like the dog he is.

Brett studied his Colt. His mother had always hated the cold weapon, hated the need for it. She thought men should live together peacefully, and where there were disputes they should be resolved by the law. A wise woman, his mother. In this she was wrong though. Sometimes the law wasn't enough. Sometimes it grew corrupt. Sometimes a man had to be strong and take justice into his own hands. You could not always count on the law to protect you.

Davis Judd and Kip Lane stole from him. After taking his father's life, they'd taken the ranch and tried to murder him. Today he was going to take back his ranch and avenge his father.

"Stay here," he told Mourning Song. "If I don't return go back to your people."

She gave him a long look. She brought her horse around in a slow circle so she was beside him, but facing in the opposite direction. Her dark eyes captured his. She leaned in and took hold of his hands.

"Be strong. Return to me," she said. Brett felt the warmth of her breath on his mouth. She shut her eyes and leaned in closer yet until her soft lips found his.

At first her kiss was gentle, then it grew steadily harder. It burned like liquid fire. Brett wrapped her in his arms and drew her close, pressing his own lips firm against hers.

Slowly, the kiss lessened and she withdrew. Brett felt as if he'd been struck by lightning. His heart pounded and his hands felt shaky.

Mourning Song grinned. "Return to me," she repeated.

"I've got to go," Brett said after catching his breath.

"I pray," she said. She got down off her horse and took a bit of dried sage from her bags. She closed her eyes and knelt down on a dyed wool blanket. Then she held the sage up against her mouth and began chanting.

Somewhat lightheaded, Brett started toward town. He tried to sweep thoughts of Mourning Song from his mind.

What had that been about though? Why did she kiss me like that?

Not so long ago she'd despised him. Red Elk had even warned him that she might try to kill him. Over time she'd gradually warmed to him, he knew that much, and it pleased him.

But she'd certainly never acted like this before. There had been a hunger in her kiss. Did she truly feel something for him or had she been merely caught up in the moment? Brett didn't know how he felt about her. Certainly, he cared for her, but he'd all but promised himself to Lisa. She was his future. Wasn't she?

Brett banished all such thoughts as he wound down through the scattered homes along the outskirts of Pryor. He was riding on Main Street before he knew it; the first man he saw was the new Sheriff, Jason Wills.

Davis Judd's man.

The fat man's eyes widened. He started to open his mouth, but Brett spoke first.

"Sheriff I don't believe your services are needed today," he said.

"Well...I," Wills fidgeted.

"In fact it might be best if you just left town. Today I'm running Davis Judd out and if you happened to be around I might just decide to shoot you."

"Big talk," Wills said. "Davis Judd will—"

Brett drew his Colt.

Wills hadn't so much as moved. The big man blinked once; he looked down the long barrel of the Colt and then started to nod.

"You've got five minutes to get on your horse and make tracks for Sheridan."

"Five minutes...why that isn't enough time."

"Drop your gun before you go." Brett brought the Colt up to eye level and sighted on the Sheriff's star. "Leave that too."

"Now see here, I'm the duly appo—"

The Colt's hammer came back with a deadly click.

Wills unbuckled his gunbelt and let it fall where he stood; he tore at the badge like it was a rattler until his shirt ripped and the star fell in the dusty street.

"Four minutes," Brett said.

Three minutes later Jason Wills was spurring his horse eastward as fast as the frightened beast would carry him.

"One down," Brett said to himself.

He started Cimarron down the street to Judd's freight office. It seemed like the best place to start looking. A skinny man in store-bought clothes leaned on one of the posts outside. Brett dismounted. He tied Cimarron at the hitching post across the street then started over.

"Davis Judd in there?" Brett asked as he approached.

The man studied Brett for a moment. "What's it to ya?"

"I've come to kill him."

At first the man only looked confused, then his eyes bulged and he paled a little. He stepped away from the post, moving into Brett's path, and then there was less than a yard separating them. "I don't know who you think you are mister but—"

In one quick motion Brett drew his gun and slammed the barrel down across the man's forehead. Like a stone, the Judd man dropped.

"Thanks. I'll look inside for myself."

He climbed the three short steps to the freight office's covered porch. Then, with all the strength he could bring to bear, he kicked the door in. The wooden frame cracked and shattered and the door swung inward. Three stunned men stood inside. Brett leveled his Colt at them.

"Davis Judd. Where is he?" he asked. "Answer or you'll get what he got." Brett jerked his head to indicate the downed man lying in the dusty street behind him.

"He's staying at the hotel," a spectacled man said. He licked his mouth nervously. "Please, I'm just a simple storekeeper."

"Well thank you," Brett said. "Now all three of you drop your guns."

"I don't have one," the storekeeper stammered.

"C'mon we can take him. He can't get all of us," a greasy looking fellow in a once-yellow shirt growled.

Brett drew the second gun from behind his belt. He stuck it against the greasy man's nose.

"Maybe not, but I promise you'll die first."

Suddenly the greasy man's eyes were very still. He swallowed. Sweat beaded up on his forehead.

"Now, I said drop those guns," Brett growled.

Slowly, very slowly, they eased their gunbelts off.

"Good, now let's put you three inside that cage you got around the back. Grab the keys storekeep."

When he had all three locked up he headed out the front door. The first man was still out cold on the front step. There was a watering trough nearby and Brett tossed the cage's key in the gray water. He walked toward the hotel. In the middle of the dusty street out front he stopped.

A number of men and women were on the street now, most busy trying hard to avoid looking at him. They spoke to each other in low, quick voices while stealing glances at Brett or the man lying unconscious in front of the freight office. He could feel the weight of their eyes.

"DAVIS JUDD," Brett roared. "YOU MURDERED MY FATHER JUDD AND I'M HERE TO SEE YOU PAY."

Men looked out at him from the hotel's dust-covered windows. The street emptied in a rush of slamming doors and running feet as the townsfolk piled into Pryor's shops and businesses. Faces lined every window. The town was silent. A Street over a dog barked.

"DAVIS JUDD. COME OUT YOU YELLOW COWARD."

"No need for that son," a voice called from behind him. "Now why don't you just shuck those guns of yours."

Slowly, Brett turned just enough to see John Hollande standing on the boardwalk behind him, a scattergun held at waist level. Hollande was smiling.

"You didn't think we expected you after last night?" he said. "You played hell for those boys I'll give you that. Now go ahead and drop your guns."

"Your boss must be awful afraid of me to send you out here. That your usual way. Sneak up behind a man?"

Hollande chuckled. "Davis Judd isn't afraid of any man."

"I won't need these to give you a whipping."

Hollande laughed harder now. "Pup, you've never seen the day you could lick me."

Brett shrugged. He unfastened his gunbelt and let his weapons fall. "Care to see about that."

Hollande was a big powerful bull of a man, but Brett was no slouch himself. He'd put on thick slabs of muscle due to living in the mountains chopping his own wood and wrestling steers. He was sure he was in better condition than Hollande. All he needed to do was wear the big man down. He could outlast him.

"I've killed better men than you with these hands." Hollande.

"Not better than me," Brett smiled. "You afraid I'll take you apart piece by piece?"

Hollande's face reddened. "Tempting, but why take a chance?" The big man brought the scattergun up to his shoulder. "Looks like your luck's run—"

A gun crashed to Brett's right and Hollande spun around until he faced away from Brett. There was a round black hole through his shirt pocket and a huge patch of blood covered the middle of his back. He fell. The scattergun struck the ground, went off; smoke and loose dirt flew from the end of it. Then Hollande was face down in the street.

Brett scrambled to get retrieve his pistols. He didn't know who else had taken a hand in this, but he wanted to find out with his guns ready.

Footsteps came from beside the hotel. A shadow appeared, and then a man in buckskins stepped out.

"We meet again, little brother," Red Elk said.

"Red Elk? How?"

The Crow grinned. "The Spirits have brought me to you."

"How did you escape all those men in the mountains? I've been all over that part of the ranch there was no way out where you led them."

"There was no way out on horseback. I led them on until dark and then set my horse loose and climbed out on foot," Red Elk said.

Brett thought about those steep granite walls. There were a few places it could be done.

But in the dark with armed men hunting me? I wouldn't even try it.

"What about your good death?"

"You are young yet," Red Elk patted him on the shoulder. Then he looked at the dead man in the street. "There will be plenty of time for you to find me a good death."

"Mourning Song is praying up on the hill to the west."

"You need my help to finish?" he said.

"I've got to see this to the end myself," Brett said. He couldn't ask Red Elk to fight his battles for him.

"You have grown strong indeed," Red Elk said with a nod. "Now you must use your strength wisely."

Without another word, the Crow mounted his horse and rode out. Brett watched him go then he turned back to the hotel.

"COME OUT JUDD. HOLLANDE IS DEAD. LET'S END THIS NOW."

The air in the street was still and heavy like an open bear trap. A fine alkali dust hung all around, motes catching the sunlight like a thousand tiny mirrors.

Slowly, the hotel door opened. Brett heard the shuffling of feet inside until Davis Judd himself stepped out of the doorway. Hatless, he wore a white shirt with the sleeves rolled up to his elbows. He looked relaxed, confident. His gun was tied down low.

"I don't know who you think you are young man," Davis said. "But I—"

Brett cut him off, "I'm Brett Rawlins, son of Betsy and Jim, who you murdered and made to look like he hung himself. And now I'm going to kill you."

"What do you think this is boy?" Davis said. His face flushed red and bright. He looked at the fallen Hollande and started walking to the end of the street. "This is a hard land. It takes strength to tame a land like this. Like most men, your father was weak. He met the land and it broke him. He couldn't face the challenge."

"And you can? You may be strong, but you waste that strength. You take all and care only for yourself."

"And what of you boy? Are you strong enough to tame Wyoming? Your friends are leaving, their wagons rolling out as we speak. They too are weak. You've surrounded yourself with weakness," Davis sneered. He smiled that wolf's grin of his. "Kill me and another just like me will ride in here, and you'll lose your ranch again within a month. You are nothing, less than nothing."

"If the Mormons are so weak why did you fear them enough to run them out? They weren't a danger to you."

"That wasn't me," Davis laughed. "That was all Kip. He hates them. That church of theirs cast him out years ago. Can't have too many boys running around you see. It complicates things for those lecherous old men."

Steps rang out on the boardwalk then. They were to Brett's left and he dare not take his eyes off Davis. For his part Judd smiled even more coldly now. He squinted at Brett and cocked his head to one side.

"Telling my secrets are you?" an oily voice said.

"Good of you to join us," Judd said. "Now finish what you started and kill this boy for me."

The footsteps continued until Brett spotted movement out of the corner of his eye. He shifted a half-step without letting his eyes leave Judd.

Kip Lane sauntered up the boardwalk like a great cat, dapper as usual, with a lit cigarette in one hand and his pistol in the other. When he reached the hotel he leaned against one of the awning posts near the door. Men parted all around him, but he paid them no mind.

"I think not Judd," Lane said. "I think this is where I quit. I've decided to start my own outfit. After all, I agree completely with you, to the strongest go the spoils. Don't mind me though. I'm only here to watch. I'll settle up with whichever of you wins." He holstered his pistol and puffed on the cigarette.

"Why you ungrateful," Davis started and then drew.

Brett couldn't believe how fast the rancher was. His own draw was just as quick, but with his sudden start Judd fired first. The shot was rushed. The bullet went low into the ground between them. Brett fired once, then again, and Judd jerked with both shots as if he'd been struck by a hammer.

Two splotches of bright crimson colored his shirt near his heart.

Judd's pistol started to rise again. Brett snapped off a third round.

Then the rancher fell face down and was still. Brett holstered his Colt.

"Well that wasn't too bad. Davis was always pretty fast," Kip crooned. He stepped over to Judd and nudged the body with his boot. Then he drew his pistol and shot the dead man twice more. "Course you won't beat me. Why I never saw the day—"

Brett drew. His left hand moved impossibly fast and the Colt snapped up clean and smooth. Like a serpent's strike, Lane's gun sprang up. Fire blossomed from its barrel, but Brett was already shooting. His first bullet took Lane in the shoulder and spoiled the gunman's aim. Brett corrected and the next two hit the outlaw dead center.

Lane's gun spilled from his hand. "You beat me. No one can beat me. You're a nobody. Just some ranch kid. I can't..."

Kip Lane collapsed in a heap. Blood soaked into the dust under him.

Brett reloaded his pistol. It had been a near thing. He'd felt the wind from Lane's bullet. He felt no pity looking down at the bodies. No more pity than he would have had for a pair of wolves he killed while they stalked after his calves.

A dark-haired woman was in the street suddenly. Allie. She ran to the bodies and stared down at the fallen Lane. She spit on Lane's handsome face. Then she stepped over him and came to Brett.

"Thank God you got him, Brett. He held me against my will. He told me he'd kill my parents if I didn't betray you," she said.

"I saw you with him," Brett said.

"What?" Allie's eyes widened. "No, that can't be. I was never with him. Not really. He said he'd kill my—"

"I saw you at the ranch the day after I climbed out of that hole you left me to die in. I was behind the barn coming to rescue you. Only you came out and then you were kissing him," Brett's voice was cold as winter wind over the high peaks.

"No," she shook her head. The bruises on her face and neck were faded, but her eyes were red and bloodshot.

"Then I found you beside the saloon that night. You sent them all after me. You lied and said I hurt you. 'A good, weak little boy' you called me."

Allie took a step back. Her eyes darted left and right like a frightened animal. "He promised he'd take me with him. I thought he was strong. He told me you were weak, but he was wrong. You're the strong one. You're the one for me and now together we can go anywhere we want. You've got the ranch and everything."

"Go with you? Allie I never want to see you again," Brett turned to get Cimarron. Despite the pain and heartache she'd caused him, saying her name still hurt.

"Brett, please no. Please." Allie stood alone in the center of the street.

Brett climbed onto the red stallion. He spoke to the men and women watching him. A few brave souls had left the buildings and come out to see better. "This is over now. Tell any Judd men you see to get out of town. There's no one left to pay their wages, and if I see them I'll shoot on sight."

————

BETWEEN YOUNGSTON and the mountains lay a long, low ridge running just a little east of town. The ridge wasn't much in the way of elevation, but from the top a mounted man could easily look down into the village.

Brett turned off the main trail from Pryor and followed the skyline up to the ridge's crest. He brought Cimarron to a stop. Faint tendrils of smoke wafted up from the burned-out hulks of houses and barns. The Sweeney's was the nearest. Along with his sons, Gideon directed the loading of their wagon with the last few items from the house.

There were other families doing the same, but more were already loaded. A few of these saw him on the skyline and pointed.

Brett wondered what they saw. With the bright sun high and the mix of blue Wyoming sky and gray Bighorns rising up behind him, they wouldn't be able to make out his features. Some might recognize the huge red horse. But what of it?

If they know who I am does that change what they see? Do they see me as some angelic avenger or as the root of all this wickedness?

By rights he should ride down and tell them the danger was past and they could stay now. With Davis Judd and Kip Lane gone there were no more threats.

But is that true?

Other men will come, Judd had said. Brett knew he was right. Some would be better than Judd, others worse. It would be years before they stopped coming, if they ever did, and even then they would only switch tactics; from using guns and violence they would switch to slippery lawyers, biased judges, corrupt politicians.

In a way Davis Judd had been right. Wyoming was a hard land and it would take great men to tame it. Gideon Sweeney was a great man true enough, strong enough in his own way. It took courage and strength to raise a family and settle in the desert only to then head out for a chance at a better life in a second untamed country. But Gideon lacked something. He did not have the will to fight his fellow man and defend what was his. He was a peaceful man suited to a peaceful land.

Rather than just strength it took a willingness to use violence when called upon. Not as Judd had—using his power only to enrich himself—or like Kip Lane who'd used his abilities for cruelty and hate. Both brought their strength to bear only as it benefited themselves. No, it took strength and wisdom in equal measure to fight for justice and protect the weak.

Was that what Red Elk meant about using my strength wisely?

Brett looked over his shoulder back toward the mountains. His father's house lay almost due east of here and, on a rolling grassy hill toward the ranch, Red Elk and Mourning Song sat their horses, watching him. The wind blew from the north just a little and Mourning Song's hair lifted in it, loose and free.

He patted Cimarron on the neck and thought about the story

she'd told that night. Brother wolf and the Great Spirit and the coming of the elk.

I thought to become a wolf like Kip Lane and Davis Judd. I thought to grow strong like them, but it isn't the wolf that's strong. The true strength is in the elk. Through starvation, blizzard, and fire the elk endure. Unyielding, they face their enemies in endless struggle.

After killing Davis Judd and Kip Lane, he'd returned to his friends but hadn't spoken. His mind was conflicted with a dozen different thoughts all at once and in all directions. He'd been trying to get his ranch back for so long and now he had it.

My ranch.

He wasn't sure when he'd started thinking of it as his own rather than his father's. When had the change taken place? He'd been thinking of Cimarron as his for months now and the big Colt revolver even longer. With the Colt he knew the exact moment.

Back in Sheridan after I killed that cowboy. That day, more than any other, had changed him. *That day I started down the path that brought me here.*

Lisa Sweeney came out of her father's house carrying a wrapped bundle. She handed it to one of her older brothers, and he placed it on their wagon, near the top of the pile. Then he climbed down and tossed a pair of ropes over the load.

I've only brought these people pain.

Kip Lane may have hated them for his own reasons, but Brett knew some of the responsibility for Youngston's fate was his. The charred skeletons of homes and structures, the family members they'd lost to Kip Lane's bullets. He was responsible for it. With Davis Judd's gold he'd tried making amends. Gold couldn't give them their lost loved ones back though.

Lisa saw him and stopped to look.

Brett didn't move. Suddenly he wasn't sure what he wanted. He drew his Colt and studied it. Such a strange thing. An instrument of steel and wood and powder, odd that such a small thing could change the fates of so many.

He could go with them. He could ride down to Lisa and go with them back to the Salt Lake and live among their people. He'd promised Lisa he would go to her. They'd have to go west and live among her people. Lisa wasn't for Wyoming. In the desert too, there would be wolves, but he wouldn't have to kill again. He could marry Lisa and be an ordinary farmer and then the law would be responsible to protect them.

Or I can stay.

He could go back to his ranch and set about rebuilding. Wyoming needed men like him. Men willing to stand up for what was right and just. He would almost certainly have to fight again, to kill again.

Brett looked from Lisa, then back toward Red Elk, his ranch, Mourning Song.

He holstered his Colt. Then he gave Lisa a single wave. She returned it, jumping up and down in excitement.

Then he swung Cimarron off the ridge toward home and Mourning Song. She loved him he knew. He'd known it since that night he found her crying at their campfire. He'd known then too that he felt things for her that he would never feel for Lisa Sweeney. Lisa was a perfect summer day, fair, brief in passing, free from worry and care. Mourning Song though. She was something else entirely, a river, deep and wide, at times serene, at other times bucking with torrential power. He could not leave her.

Mourning Song saw him coming and spurred her palomino. She met him halfway.

Brett looked into her dark eyes. "I love you," he said and meant it.

She smiled and nodded. She held a hand over her heart. "I love you," she said.

Brett brought Cimarron close to her. He leaned closer. She came forward to meet him.

"We are going home now?" Red Elk interrupted.

"We are," Brett said.

"Good, I haven't eaten in a day or two. Mourning Song can cook me something. She's much better at it than her grandmother."

"Her grandmother?"

"Yes," Red Elk gave her an appraising look. "As I said she's half Crow on her mother's side. Her grandmother was captured in a raid."

"You said your first wife couldn't cook," Brett said. "Wasn't she captured by the Cheyenne in a raid?"

And if she were pregnant when the Cheyenne took her.

Red Elk only smiled.

Brett marveled at his quiet friend. *All this time, all these months. Not when we freed her. Not even when he was giving his life to save us. He never said anything.* In the end Brett could only shake his head and smile back.

Does it matter? We are all together now.

Tomorrow they would start rebuilding their ranch; tomorrow he and Mourning Song would begin their life together. He took her in his arms, drew her close, and kissed her.

<<<<>>>>

AFTERWORD

Thank you for reading Blood on the Bighorns. I hope you enjoyed yourself. To receive updates about new releases please subscribe to my email list at:

http://eepurl.com/b5EQJb

If you haven't already please enjoy the first chapter of my previous western
Sonoran Gold

SONORAN GOLD

CHAPTER ONE

"REBECCA, CAN YOU BELIEVE THIS?" In his calloused palm, Saul
Lafleur held a sparkling yellow nugget the size of a robin's egg. His
smile was broad and white and gleaming. "This changes
everything."

Rebecca smiled back at her husband. "I can hardly imagine it.
You've worked so hard for this." She leaned down to see the gold
better, and Saul felt her soft fingers caressing the back of his hand.

"There are more," Saul said, "many more." He tossed an open
canvas bag onto the kitchen table and nuggets rolled and rattled out
like gamblers' dice. He swept Rebecca up in his arms and kissed her,
squeezing her tight around her narrow waist.

"Fool man," she said with a playful grin. She spread her hands
over his broad chest. "You didn't even wash off. You'll ruin my
good apron."

Saul released her and laughed a deep, happy rumble. He offered
her a mock bow. "Becca, I'll buy you a hundred aprons—a thousand

—or I'll hire a cook with her own aprons. The ore's so rich you'll never need to cook again."

"Saul Lafleur," Rebecca said. She whisked a white ovencloth at him. "You will do no such thing, you know how I like to cook."

A dark-haired boy of seven darted into the room, joining them. The boy had Saul's strong features and his mother's dark hair and eyes. "Papa, Papa, you're home!" he cried. He wrapped both sun-browned arms around Saul's middle.

"I am home, Jim, and look." Saul knelt down to the boy's eye level. Then he held up the nugget to his son. "I found this."

Hesitating only for a moment, Jim reached for it. He pinched it between his fingers and held it up against the afternoon light. He squinted as he examined it.

"What is it, Papa?"

"Gold. I found it this morning, and many more besides."

"It's shiny. Can I keep it?"

"You can keep as many as you like, son," Saul smiled. "Keep it safe, though. Gold isn't easy to come by and it's tougher still to keep."

Jim nodded. "I'll keep it safe." Almost reverently, he held his pants pocket open with one hand, and then placed the nugget deep inside with the other. He looked back to Saul. "I found a rabbit by the spring today. I tried to catch him, but he ran into some thorns." The boy held up his elbow to show off a set of shallow scratches on the back of his arm.

Saul laughed. In Arizona in the heart of the Sonora desert, every-thing had thorns. Thorns, spines, thistles, or barbs—there was no avoiding them. He still remembered his own adventures with bruises and scratches at Jim's age, and Virginia had been a far more gentle land than this.

"You'll have to be quick to catch a rabbit out here," Saul said. "It takes an uncanny smart one to survive all the coyotes and bobcats."

He rose and moved to the cabin's open door. The evening breeze was starting to cool, and it smelled of sweet desert blooms. To the distant north, a line of red-and-purple-tinted clouds rode the winds. *Fair-weather clouds*, his father would have called them. They offered nothing more than a passing of temporary shade. Closer to the cabin, the tall saguaro and clumpy prickly pear took on a warm orange glow. A few birds whistled and warbled, seemingly relieved for the end of another scorching Sonoran day.

With the ore they'd found this morning, they could finally afford something better than the little dirt-floored cabin on the north end of the Santa Catalinas. He could build Rebecca a real house, with a real floor of polished wood. One close to Tucson, where Jim could go and get the schooling he needed.

The sun dipped low, sending out a few shafts of dying gold, then was gone. Saul closed the door.

Near the kitchen stood a little table and four chairs. Saul took one and leaned his tired arms on the tabletop. He watched Rebecca working at the stove. She lifted the heavy cast iron skillet from the fire, set it aside, and then fanned her small cloth over the biscuits to cool them. He marveled at her. He'd just told his wife that after five years of struggling, five years of digging, five years of barely scratching out a living in this hot, god-forsaken place, he'd finally found the fortune he had always known was here.

The Lost Escalante Mine, the Iron Door Mine—the place had other names, as well. After the owners had vanished during an Apache massacre, hundreds of treasure seekers had gone searching for it.

And he'd been the one to find it.

He'd long believed in the lost mine since before coming to Arizona—even back East the stories were spread far and wide—but his purpose had never been to find it. He wasn't some fool treasure hunter. Finding buried treasure was always a long shot, as often it never existed at all.

No, his plan had been to start a mine of his own. The hills and mountains of Arizona were rich in minerals, both silver and gold. They said anyone could get them. Anyone willing to settle in the desert. Anyone willing to brave the Apaches. Anyone willing to dig down deep enough.

After wasting four years sinking his own shaft into the mountain with only an ounce or two of fickle color to show for it, he'd been on the verge of quitting. Finally, almost on a whim, he'd decided to investigate a pile of rubble nearer his claim's base. A hot afternoon of digging had revealed a broken miner's axe, and he'd decided to clear away the rubble and see what was beneath. He'd found more wreckage, a few lamps and shovels, and then a caved-in shaft almost fifty feet into the mountain. There was another cave-in further down, and it had taken himself and a neighbor another week to shore it up and clear away the boulders. By then he'd known it was the Lost Escalante.

Just that morning, he and the neighbor, Pat Davies, had finally broken through, and after exploring deeper, they'd found the exposed ore.

Saul's heart had leapt when he'd spied the glistening ore winking at him from the dark. He knew he could never prove that this was the legendary lost mine of the Santa Catalinas. In truth, he didn't care to try. He'd found gold, and that's all that mattered. His struggling family was now rich beyond belief. The vein ran wide as his hand and spanned over six feet, floor-to-ceiling, with dozens of smaller veins spiderwebbing off in all directions.

The mine would take years to develop fully. It might not even happen in his own lifetime. Jim would have to carry on the work.

Saul looked for his son. Jim was playing on the floor now. He wondered at how quickly his boyish mind could switch from shiny yellow rocks, to rabbits, and then on to the next thing. Rebecca's older brother had carved him a set of blocks with a combination of letters and numbers on them before they came West; Jim was playing with them now, arranging them one atop the other.

The discovery at the mine would change everything. Jim would have a future he never could have imagined otherwise. He could go to law school back East, become educated, respected. Saul's own father had been a poor coal miner in Virginia, a man who rose early, worked hard, attended church regularly, and never came back from the war. Rebecca's brother had served under him, a gangly kid from Carolina who'd lied about his age so he could enlist. Out of their unit, only two men survived to the war's end—Rebecca's brother and a young lieutenant.

"Saul..." Rebecca's voice broke through his thoughts.

"Sorry, must have drifted off. What is it, dear?"

"Saul, there's a rider coming. Did you invite someone to dinner?"

"I invited Pat over to discuss the future. We have to hire more men. We'll need timber to shore up the main shaft and more powder for blasting, bits and tools as well. I'll have to get Osweiller at the bank to loan us the cash to get by. But with this," Saul held up a nugget, "he'll have no choice but to give us what we need."

"I don't like him. Pat, I mean," Rebecca said. Her eyes narrowed. "I don't like the way he looks at me."

"Dear heart, I know you don't like him. I need him, though, and he's stuck with me through thick and thin. He knows much more of hard rock mining than I." Saul rose and put his hands on his wife's shoulders. "I promise I'll keep it quick."

A few minutes later, a knock came at the door. Before Saul could open it, Jim sprang up to get it. He swung the door open.

"Thank you, young man." Davies took off his hat and bowed as he entered.

"Did you see my shiny rock, Mister Pat?" Jim drew out the nugget for examination.

"Well, there's a lot more where that came from, young Jim. I'll wager we can bring you an even bigger one tomorrow," Pat said. He patted the boy on the head.

Saul didn't miss the disapproving look from Rebecca. Her knuckles had gone white around the stirring spoon. "Jim, go and get me a pail of water from the pump," she said.

"Pat, please have a seat," Saul said. "I was just making a list and adding up a few figures in my head. I'll have to go to the bank tomorrow and take out a loan for supplies."

"Well, that's what I've come to talk about, Saul."

"Good, you've given it some thought as well, then. I knew I could count on you, Pat."

Without another word, Pat drew his pistol.

"Pat, what...?" Saul saw the spark down the long, black bore. He felt the bullet hammer into his chest. He sprawled back out of his chair and crashed to the dirt floor.

Even through the ringing in his ears, Saul heard the hammer click back again.

Rebecca had started to scream. "Run, Jim, RUN AND HIDE!"

Saul could see his wife's legs and the edge of her blue patterned dress. It was frayed at the hem. No matter. He'd buy her another one soon enough. He tried to turn his head, but something was wrong with his neck. It didn't hurt, but he couldn't move it. He yelled, and only a thin gurgling sound came out. He smelled burnt powder.

Rebecca was crying; something had upset her. He needed to help her. He needed to get to his feet and comfort his love.

Another shot rang out, and then Rebecca fell silent. Saul could see her clearly then. She lay on the floor near the stove, her long, black hair masking her face. There was a small black hole in her lower chest. A trickle of blood poured out of it onto her white apron, and she was still.

One of the nuggets had spilled from the table. It lay just inches from Saul's face. His eyes locked on the gleaming rock. His future, everything he'd ever worked or prayed for, it was all right there, ripe for the picking. He could buy Rebecca a house in town. One with a little white picket fence out front and a big window overlooking the mountains and a yard where Jim could play. She loved to cook, and she loved the look of the mountains in the evenings.

"Sorry, partner," Pat said as his dirt-stained fingers reached down around the nugget. "I just can't let a chance like this slip away."

Saul heard the hammer click back one final time. He looked back at Rebecca. Her face was still masked by her thick hair. Her right hand lay before her, stretched out and open as if she were reaching for him. He forced his eyes to focus on the tiny band of gold he'd put on her finger they day they'd married back in Virginia. They'd been so happy. Then he heard nothing more.

\#

A big black horse with a wicked eye carried Reuben Jacobs into

Tucson. He'd stolen it from a ranch near Tascosa months ago, and the horse had proven a good one over the long miles since. There wasn't an ounce of quit in him. The black could go all day at a pace few others could match.

Sweat rolled down Reuben's back and vanished into his faded blue shirt. With dark, narrowed eyes, he studied the town as he passed through the dusty streets.

The town was crowded despite the incredible heat. There were a few hotels—two-story wooden structures—but most of the other buildings were Arizona's traditional white stucco over adobe. The roofs were flat. Reuben wondered about how they would shed the rain.

Doubtful they even think about it. Rain was beyond rare in this part of the country.

The Sonoran Desert wasn't a hospitable place, though men certainly could scratch out a life here. They grew oranges and wheat and corn and other crops near the desert's few rivers, the Salt and Gila, using hand-dug canals for the water they needed. But it was gold that really drew men here, silver and gold. There were rich veins to the south around Tombstone and a few off in the Santa Catalinas.

In a way, it was gold that had drawn Reuben Jacobs here, too. A shipment of gold, to be exact. Seventy thousand dollars' worth. That kind of gold could change a man's life.

He stabled his horse after choosing to stay in the hotel nearest to Tucson's bank, the Grand Nelson. The owner, Nelson himself, met him inside. His eyes were bloodshot and his breath reeked of cheap whiskey. "Name?" he asked from behind the registry.

"Texas Jack." There were a lot of Texas Jacks out West; Reuben knew at least a half-dozen.

"How many nights, sir?" If Nelson had any qualms about him using an obviously fake name, he gave no sign of it. *Probably used to it by now, or too drunk to care.* For all the coming of the rail and the iron horse and civilization to tame the West, Tucson was still a rough town. Gold always attracted a rough breed of men. Men who never used their real names.

"Two at least. Though it might take more."

"Two bits a day, not including meals or laundry. If you need more days, just let me know. I'll be right here." Nelson handed him a key with the number 204 stamped into the handle. He slumped down at his desk, and his eyes shifted to a half-empty bottle by his elbow.

Carrying his saddlebags and gear, Reuben climbed the stairs. After stowing them, he washed his face in a shallow tin basin. The water was warm, but it felt good to be free of the grime and dust. His room had a window facing Tucson's main street. A loose curtain hung there. The edges were a bold red, but the desert sun had long ago faded the center to a pale pink. Reuben moved the thin fabric aside and looked across the street.

Reuben shaved. If all went as planned, it would be several days before he had another chance. He studied his reflection as he finished up. His eyes were black with scattered flecks of amber and, other than a few wild wisps of gray, his hair matched them. His face was also tinted a deep brown except where his hat covered it. Done shaving, he left a slim mustache, but there were scissors on the table and he trimmed away the longest hairs.

The sun was low against the horizon when he finished and headed out to eat. He paused under the hotel's awning and studied the bank. There were two men on the roof now, each with repeating rifles, and another stationed on a bench covering the front door. An orange glow flared bright as one of the men on the roof pulled on his cigarette. Reuben turned and started for a busier stretch of town.

He'd just stepped off the boardwalk into the shadowed gap between the hotel and the Western Rose saloon when a voice called out.

"Where'd you steal that horse?"

Reuben froze. "You are mistaken, friend," he replied coolly. "I bought him off a rancher near Austin."

"And I suppose you weren't riding him when you robbed the stage between Lincoln county and Santa Fe, or when you held up the First American bank in Durango."

"You must have me confused with someone else. I've never been to Durango."

A blond man stepped out of the dark. His hair was trimmed tight and slicked back around his ears, and he wore a tall brown hat with a short, flat brim. He smiled and clapped Reuben on the shoulder. "Good to see you, Reuben."

Reuben shook his friend's hand. "Ben, you got my message."

"I did. That the bank?" Ben leaned out to peer at the guarded building.

"It is. But we can talk more later. You know somewhere to eat?"

"There's a mex place a few streets over. They're open late and it's quiet."

"Lead the way."

Ten years Reuben had known Ben Heath. They'd pulled a few jobs together—a stage holdup outside of Denver, another up in Cheyenne, and then they'd robbed a bank in Nevada before going their separate ways. Ben had wanted to go honest, and he'd started a ranch in Northern California to supply the mines. The ranch had folded when the gold fields panned out; the bank foreclosed, and Ben had quickly fallen back into his outlaw ways. He'd held up a few stages and gotten away clean, but the truth was that what they did was getting harder. Civilization had come West, and with it had come law and order. The lawmen were getting organized. It was impossible now to escape the law by running from county to county or even state to state. Lawmen cooperated and curried favors with one another. A warrant in Texas could easily be served in New Mexico.

Ben led them through town to a little hole-in-the-wall place. There were only three tables inside, all empty, and they took one near the back.

The waitress brought them warm tortillas, bowls of rice, thin-cut steak, and a mixture of sweet yellow corn and black beans. They ate like men who'd gone weeks without; good food was rare in their line of work.

Reuben rolled the tortilla up and ran it over his empty plate, soaking up the little grease that remained. It had been three days since he'd eaten anything but his own cooking, and he'd never been much hand in that regard.

"The bank is out," Reuben started once he'd finished. "Too well guarded, and half of Tucson would like nothing more than to take a shot at an outlaw. How many men do you have?"

"Five, including you and me. Curley Tim and Tocho, the man you sent. Dave Nelson you don't know. He don't look like much, but he's solid."

"I didn't want Curley Tim. I warned you about him." Reuben didn't like the man. He was unpredictable and often violent, though Ben was good at curbing his tendencies.

"I'll keep a tight rein on him," Ben said. As much as Reuben liked Ben, the man had a soft spot for his fool cousin. "You sure there's no way to hit the bank?"

"Four men at least guarding the bank. All armed with rifles. We'd never get in without waking the town, and even then, there's no way to get back out. We'd be cut to pieces before we made three blocks. Daytime is even worse."

"All right. So what is the plan, then?" Ben asked.

"We know where the gold is headed. We know the route it will have to take. We'll hit it along the trail." Reuben never really expected the bank to be an option. Too many factors beyond his control. Too much risk.

"That won't be easy. Have you seen the wagon?"

"No," Reuben said.

"It's impressive. Formidable, even. Armored sides and top, room for four armed men and firing ports. It takes six mules to pull the thing," Ben said. He shook his head. "I don't know if it can be done. That doesn't even take the outriders into account. Rumor is this Pat Davies has hired twenty armed guards to ride along."

"Formidable," Reuben chuckled. "No one said taking seventy thousand in gold was going to be easy."

"I'm getting too old for this sort of thing. It was fun when I was in my twenties, but now it's time to let this life go." Ben took off his hat and ran his fingers over his greasy blond hair.

Reuben picked up Ben's hat. As much as he didn't care to admit it, Ben was right. Though both were still on the uphill side of forty, neither had the stomach for this kind of life anymore. They'd been lucky so far, but the odds were getting ever higher against the life they led. Sooner or later they'd catch a rope or a bullet.

"That is the plan," Reuben said. "One last big score and then..."

"And then?"

"Respectability. Settling down somewhere." Reuben spun the hat in his hands. He ran a finger along the long white-and-black banded feather Ben had tucked into the band. "I can't believe no one has shot this thing off your head yet."

Ben snatched the hat out of Reuben's hands. "Don't insult my hat. An old Cherokee medicine man said that as long as I keep that eagle feather in it I was immune to bullets. Immune."

"I still say it's a turkey feather, but you keep thinking that, pard," Reuben smiled. "If we pull this off without catching lead, I'll stick one in my own hat." He took a drink and then pushed back his chair. "You staying in the hotel?"

"No, up in the hills with the boys. I kept them out of town like you asked."

"Good. It wouldn't do to have them hanging around Tucson. We're going to need more men, though."

"I might know a couple who'd do. I'll come by tomorrow and we can see about them."

After shaking Ben's hand again, Reuben started back to the hotel. The town was nearly silent now, the only noise drifting from a few saloons scattered along the main street. On impulse and against his better judgment, he stopped into the Western Rose for a drink.

The saloon was full, every table packed with gamblers, rattling dice, whiskey, and playing cards. Reuben found a narrow gap at the bar between a pair of miners and squeezed in. The bartender, a broad-shouldered man with an easy smile, found him and leaned over, cupping one ear.

"Whiskey," he said over the steady roar of the crowd.

The man returned with his drink and Reuben paid for it. He

wouldn't have more than one; he'd never been a heavy drinker. He put his back to the bar to study the crowd.

In a way, every Western town was the same. There were the usual miners, a few cowboys, a handful of professional gamblers dressed in their finest, a flock of soiled doves prospecting the crowd, and at the far end of the room at a table less crowded than the rest sat a group of four men who stood out from the others. All four of them wore their guns slung low and tied down. Like himself, the four surveyed the crowd with hunter's eyes. Reuben recognized them.

Dean Walker was a first rate gunhand. His hair was light brown and his skin very fair. He'd come from somewhere back East and made a name for himself in the live oak country around San Antonio during a vicious range war between sheepherders and the cattle ranchers. Oddly enough, he'd fought on the side of the sheepherders; usually it was the cattlemen who had the hired guns, and rumor had it he was seeing a Mexican girl at the time. Reuben had met him several times in Texas and later New Mexico and found him likable enough, but he'd heard Walker was sick now. Nothing wrong with his body, or with his gunhand—there was something broken in his mind.

The one at the table's end had a surly look to him. He was a big bull of a man, well over six foot, heavy and thick about the neck and chest and arms, and his face was covered in shaggy reddish-brown hair. Reuben had never met Braxton McClutchen personally, but there were a great deal of stories about the gunman. He'd killed eight men in the uprisings in Kansas just before the war and left two steps ahead of a noose. In the years following, he'd shot a bloody trail across a half-dozen other states.

The last man was James Tannen. His past wasn't so colorful as the others. He'd used his gun on both sides of the law. He'd been a sheriff in Missouri and later a Texas Ranger. Then he'd got into some trouble with a dancing girl and ended up working for the mines in Colorado. Of the three gunfighters, Reuben regarded him as the most dangerous.

The fourth man was dressed better than the others. He wore a black suit, and there was a matching hat and riding gloves lying on the table next to him. He was a big man, tall and solemn with clipped brown hair. His blue eyes were sharp as ice, never lingering but every bit as watchful as the better-known gunmen's. He wore a gun, as all men did, and his was tied down like the others. By the company he kept, this could only be Pat Davies, former owner of the Devil's Spit gold mine. The man Reuben planned to rob.

Putting his back to the table again, Reuben turned to the bar. He downed his shot quickly and moved toward the door. Some part of him had hoped these men would be here. He wanted to look Davies in the eye before he robbed the man blind. Now it seemed foolish— an unnecessary risk he should have avoided.

Coming here was a mistake. Better if they hadn't seen me. Better if they never see me coming.

As the door closed, he saw Tannen watching him over his drink. There was a quick gleam of recognition in the man's eye. Then Reuben was out the door and heading to the hotel.

Seventy thousand dollars was riding on this. He couldn't afford a mistake. With three gunmen—not to mention Davies himself, who was reputed to be good with a gun—and, if the rumors were true, another seventeen hired guards to ride along, even a single mistake could prove fatal.

To read more please see my book:
Sonoran Gold

Made in the USA
Las Vegas, NV
23 May 2022

49262198R00121